Worthy Opponents

DANIELLE STEEL

Worthy Opponents

A Novel

RANDOM HOUSE
LARGE PRINT

Copyright © 2023 by Danielle Steel

Published in the United States of America by Random House Large Print in association with Delacorte Press, an imprint of Random House, a division of Penguin Random House LLC, New York.

Cover image: © mila_hu/Shutterstock

The Library of Congress has established a Cataloging-in-Publication record for this title.

ISBN: 978-0-593-58789-8

www.penguinrandomhouse.com/large-print-format-books

FIRST LARGE PRINT EDITION

Printed in the United States of America

1st Printing

To my wonderful children,
Beatrix, Trevor, Todd, Nick,
Samantha, Victoria, Vanessa,
Maxx, and Zara,

May you find and love and be loved
by worthy people who make your life
bigger and better and wonderful,
beyond your greatest dreams.
May you be forever blessed in every way.

With all my love,
Mom / DS

Worthy Opponents

Chapter 1

Spencer Brooke was a small, trim woman, with a subtle but very definite sense of style. She stood out in a crowd, and was noticeably chic. She wore her blond hair in a bun at work and loose when she was at home. At thirty-seven, she ran a major enterprise. She was the owner and CEO of one of the most respected department stores in New York, Brooke and Son, more commonly known as Brooke's. Although her more distant ancestors and her mother's family had all been bankers for generations, her father's family had been in the retail business. She was the fourth generation. It was in her blood. She loved the store and everything about it, and had ever since she was a child. She loved the smell of it, of muted perfume, the moment she walked through the door, and the elegance of the merchandise they carried, which made her proud whenever she saw it.

She was fourteen years old when her grandfather, Thornton Brooke, told her that one day she would run the store. It had never occurred to her before, but from then on, she had taken special pride in it. Her grandfather was eighty years old then. He taught her the things she would need to know one day, and would later quiz her on the information he'd shared with her. Brooke's in its present form had been Thornton's dream as a young man.

Thornton's father, Jeremiah, had owned the largest, most successful department store in New York. He had established it with his own inherited fortune in 1920, with a partner. They called it Johnson and Brooke, and when Jeremiah bought out his partner a year later, he kept the name. They had the finest elite customers in the city. All of Jeremiah's male relatives before him had been bankers, and his own father was skeptical when Jeremiah founded the store with the family money he had inherited. Jeremiah had an unfailing instinct for and attraction to retail. He knew just what both men and women wanted to buy, and he supplied it, bringing in the highest quality merchandise from Europe, and beautifully designed pieces from all the luxury brands in the States.

Thornton was nine years old when suddenly everything changed. He didn't understand what had happened at first. The family moved from their mansion on Fifth Avenue to a small apartment in Gramercy Park. His grandfather's bank closed its doors, and he heard his parents speak of the closing of the store in whispers. Jeremiah gave up his beloved store nine years after he'd opened it in the same year that his son Thornton was born. Thornton was twelve when he fully understood that they had lost everything in the stock market crash of 1929, which was why Jeremiah had to lose the store and go to work at a men's haberdashery. Thornton's mother cried all the time, and his father wore a perennially grim expression from then on. The servants Thornton had grown up with had disappeared. The family had kept one maid. Meals with his parents were a silent hour of torture. Thornton couldn't wait to escape to his room. Unlike others they knew who had lost even more than they had, the family had enough to live on, in a frugal existence. They just managed to get by, but they had a roof over their heads and weren't starving. His father had looked older instantly, and suffered from ill health from then on, but went to work anyway. Even as an adult, Thornton could remember vividly how gray his father had become. Everything about him was gray, his hair, his face, the atmosphere in the house.

They had saved enough to send Thornton to college. He went to Princeton as all the men in his family had before him. He was twenty-one years old and a senior when the Japanese attacked Pearl Harbor in December 1941. Two months later, he enlisted in the army. He spent the war in Europe, and survived the invasion of Normandy. His father, Jeremiah, died of tuberculosis at fifty-seven while Thornton was away at war. He returned to find his mother looking ancient and frail, although she was only fifty. The days of glory had never come again. In his spare time during the war, Thornton dreamed of opening a store, not on the grand scale of the one they'd had, but something smaller and just as exclusive. He had no idea how he would do it, but he knew he would. He had a more outgoing, cheerful, positive personality than his parents. He came home from the war older and wiser, with a fire in his belly, and a dream.

Thornton met Hannabel Phillips six months after he got back from Europe and was released by the army. Hannabel was a beautiful, lively girl from Virginia. Thornton was mad for her. His father had left him a small amount of money. It wasn't a great deal, but it was a start. They married in 1945. She was working in an exclusive dress shop uptown in New York and had a style of her own. She had the same passion for fashion and high-quality merchandise that Thornton did. She was a year younger than Thorny, as his friends called him. She hadn't been to college, but she was a bright girl. Neither of them was afraid to disagree with the other. Thornton loved a good argument, even with his wife, and she was a worthy opponent. He had strong opinions, and he never lost sight of his dreams.

Their son, Tucker, was born on their first anniversary. There had been complications during the birth, and the doctors told them afterwards that Hannabel wouldn't be able to have other children, but she and Thornton were happy with their only son. Tucker was a strapping baby boy.

He didn't have his parents' fiery, outgoing nature, but he had an aptitude for math even as a child, and a passion for finance. He talked about being a banker or an accountant when he grew up. He learned to add and subtract before he learned to read. He had his ancestors' bankers' blood in his veins and none of the entrepreneurial "retail blood" of his grandfather Jeremiah or his father.

Tucker was a quiet child. He and his father had little in common, and Tucker barely saw him. Thorny was working two jobs during the week, and a third on the weekends. Hannabel stayed home to take care of their son, and she was clever at helping Thorny save his money. She made their clothes, upholstered their furniture, and made their curtains. Four years after Thorny had come home from the war, he had enough money to go to a bank, looking respectable and sufficiently financially sound to borrow the rest of what he needed to open a store. Twenty-one years after his father had had to close the most exclusive department store in the city, Thorny opened his own small, very elegant shop, far downtown from where his father's much larger store had been. He was thirty years old and full of great ideas. He had an instinct for men's clothing and Hannabel taught him what he needed to know about women's apparel.

The store was an instant success and turned into a goldmine. Ten years later, in 1960, he bought a large old building near his small exclusive shop in the same poor neighborhood and turned the inside into a thing of beauty. It was like a secret treasure in a place where you'd least expect it. Brooke's was an institution by then, famous for its luxurious, elegant clothes for men and women. The staff brought over the latest fashions from Europe and worked closely with high-end American designers, often influencing what they produced. Brooke's had one-of-a-kind pieces. The store was a gem, although the outside of the building itself was ugly. It was on the fringes of a marginal neighborhood, so Thorny had bought the building cheap, but no one seemed to care about the location, as he had guessed they wouldn't. Inside, the store was elegant and luxurious, and smelled of fine leather and expensive perfume. The décor was avant-garde and up-to-date. The most elegant society women in New York came from uptown to shop at Brooke's. They knew they would always find something special there, something that no one else would be wearing, handmade knits from Italy, and evening gowns from Paris. They special-ordered dresses from Brooke's own designers and bought alligator handbags in every color.

Thornton reveled in the sheer pleasure of what he did and what he sold. The merchandise in the store was known for its high quality and stylishness. He brought samples home to Hannabel sometimes to ask her advice, and she came into the store to give him her opinion on displays and merchandise. They were a team, in the most modern way, although Hannabel didn't work at the store. She didn't need to. She had an unfailing eye where fashion was concerned. Like Thornton, she knew their merchandise by heart, and she knew even better what women would want to wear next season or next year. With Hannabel's instincts and his own, Thornton built Brooke and Son into a booming business. He fully expected his son, Tucker, to come into the business with him when he graduated from

Princeton. Thorny had taken Tucker with him to Princeton as a child when he went to annual reunions. He had no trouble convincing Tucker to attend Princeton, but it was nearly impossible to get him interested in the store. Another offshoot of their gene pool ran through his veins. As he got older, the only thing that held Tucker's attention was finance. He had no choice but to comply with his father's demands. Thornton made it clear to his son at an early age that he expected him to work at the store. Tucker felt as though a life sentence in prison awaited him when he graduated. He begged to go to business school, just to postpone going to work at the store. Thornton granted him that wish, deciding that having a master's degree in business might be useful for them.

Tucker married Eileen, a girl from an extremely restrained, conservative family in Boston, who had as little interest in commerce as Tucker did himself. Her family, with old money and old-fashioned ideas, frankly disapproved of Tucker's family's involvement in a store. Tucker was working at Brooke's by then, and was embarrassed by it, and so was his wife. Tucker worked in the finance office, and Thornton could easily see him becoming CFO one day, but not CEO. Thornton jokingly said to Hannabel that he would just have to run the store himself until a grandson arrived who could run it with him. Tucker was never going to be that person. Eileen had no interest in fashion and wore dreary, conservative clothes like her mother. Everything she wore looked dowdy and shapeless. She wasn't an unattractive woman, but the style in which she dressed made her seem that way, and Tucker preferred it. They were cautious about everything, not risk-takers, and they waited until Eileen was nearly thirty-nine, and Tucker nearly forty, after twelve years of marriage, to conceive their first child. They had been in no hurry to have children, often thought of and would have preferred not having any, but finally gave in to social and familial pressure. They felt that a baby would be an intrusion on their marriage.

There was no doubt in their minds that the baby would be a son, once Eileen was pregnant. Thornton was thrilled at the prospect. They didn't even bother to consider girls' names. They were that sure that it was going to be a baby boy. Tucker hoped he'd be a banker one day, and so did Eileen, not a "shopkeeper," as she referred to her father-in-law with disdain. They decided to call him Spencer, a family name on Eileen's side. Thornton had been afraid they wouldn't have children at all and was greatly relieved at the idea of a grandson. He wanted a grandson to continue the tradition of Brooke's. Both Tucker and Eileen were shocked when told their baby was a girl. The possibility had never oc-curred to them, and they named her Spencer anyway, and were sorely disappointed.

She was beautiful without a doubt, with her white-blond hair, but she wasn't a boy. Tucker could hardly see himself painting a sign that said "Brooke and Daughter." Eileen and Tucker acted as though a misfortune had befallen them and viewed Spencer's sex as an embarrassing failure. As a result, most of the time they ignored her and left her to a nanny. They had been willing to accept a son, but not a daughter.

Spencer's grandfather adjusted to her arrival sooner than her father when he saw how bright she was. She adored her grandparents, who were warm and loving to her. Hannabel rarely left home with-out a hat with a little chic veil, and Spencer loved trying on her grandmother's hats. Her lackluster parents always acted as though there had been a mistake, and she was somebody else's child. She was so different from her parents and much more like her grandparents.

Spencer loved helping out at the store as early as in her teens. She had a proper summer job there in the stockroom at seventeen and was selling on the floor at eighteen. She followed fashion trends closely and absorbed all the information her grand-father shared with her. She remembered everything.

His words were sacred to her. She attended Parsons School of Design simultaneously with Eugene Lang College, and majored in fashion administration. After flirting briefly with the idea of becoming a designer, she decided she preferred the opportunities that the store provided her. And at her father's urging, she got her master's in business administration at Columbia.

She went to work at the store as soon as she got her graduate degree. She and her grandfather had an extraordinary first year of her working there full-time. He shared the secrets of his success in retail with her. She learned more than she'd ever dreamed she would at the feet of the master, and they had a great time together. Two of his favorite mottos were "Never be afraid of change" and "Don't get stuck in a rut just because something has always been done a certain way." He had remarkably forward, modern ideas about marketing and merchandising. He was ninety-one at the time, at the pinnacle of success, still full of energy, and always with a new idea he wanted to try. He listened to the comments made by his staff, and always found a way to blend new ideas with old ones in his own distinctive way.

Spencer's father was still CFO then, having hated every year he'd worked there, and eager to retire at sixty-six after an undistinguished career in the shadow of his father. But Spencer was still a long way from being ready to take over, and Thornton had no desire to relinquish the reins to anyone yet, not even his beloved granddaughter, who at her age still had much to learn about the business. Thornton was still having too much fun running his store to retire.

Hannabel came through frequently, always with a critical eye on the merchandise, with useful comments to make to her husband. Thornton always listened to her. She was rarely wrong. Styles had changed, but the concepts of successful retailing hadn't. Spencer learned a great deal from both of them. She loved working for her grandfather.

The idea of moving the store to a better, fancier location uptown had been discussed many times, but Thornton always rejected it. Although the neighborhood had improved in the last fifty years, it still bordered on some seedy areas. The customers who came from uptown in droves didn't seem to mind, and more than ever, Brooke's was an unexpected jewel in the midst of a dicey neighborhood, which Thornton felt gave them a certain cachet. He owned the building, and he had no desire to sell it and move. He thought it would just make the store seem ordinary if they moved uptown. It was the one point he was always adamant about, and since his instincts had always been infallible on all subjects, his advisors at the store no longer challenged him about a move. They stayed where they were, on the border of what was now Chelsea, with some tenements still nearby. The location didn't worry Thornton at all. The store was a moneymaker beyond even what Thornton had dreamed of. It was a goldmine.

No one was prepared when Thornton had a massive stroke and died in his sleep the night before his ninety-second birthday, especially Spencer, and Thornton's wife, Hannabel, even more so. She was paralyzed by grief. They'd been married for sixty-seven years. Everyone was devastated, even the employees. They closed the store out of respect the next day. Everything about Thornton Brooke and his incredible energy had suggested that he was immortal and would live forever. His sudden death had stunned them all.

Spencer couldn't imagine her life without him, and it was as though Hannabel's batteries had suddenly run out of power. She seemed lost and confused for the first time. Spencer helped her through the difficult weeks after, but her grandmother wasn't the same once Thornton died. The life had gone out of her, as Spencer realized that the love her grandparents shared had fueled both of them, and they were irreversibly joined. It was shocking to watch Hannabel go straight downhill and refuse to rally. She didn't want to live without Thornton. She didn't know how.

Tucker was equally distraught for different reasons. His father had died too soon, at ninety-two. Spencer, at twenty-six, was too young to take over, just a year out of business school, without enough experience. Tucker was desperate to get out of the business he had hated all his life, but there was no one else to step into his father's shoes, and he resented his father for it. He could see himself stuck there for many more years, and he had no desire to die in the saddle as his father had. He wanted out, and there was no way that was going to happen anytime soon. The realization that he was trapped in the job he hated depressed him profoundly.

It was a dark time for Spencer. Her grandmother had stopped coming to the store once her husband died, to the store's detriment and her own. She had two massive heart attacks within four months of Thornton's death, and died the night of the second one, which made things seem even more devastating for the senior staff, who had known the elder Brookes so well. It was the end of an era.

Tucker made a series of rapid, very poor decisions, canceling several of their more important lines, because he thought the margins weren't good enough, and as soon as he did, customers began complaining that the merchandise wasn't as exciting as it had been before Thornton's death.

Profits dropped in the first year after Thornton died, and again the second year, and Tucker refused to listen to his daughter or anyone else about the merchandise they had stopped carrying. Tucker didn't care. Spencer was the assistant fashion director of the store then, and worked under Marcy Parker, a woman who had worked at the store for thirty years. Marcy had a strong track record in marketing luxury brands, and she disagreed with everything Tucker was doing, to no avail. They had heated arguments about it, and Spencer was terrified that Marcy Parker would quit. Spencer's mother was constantly in a bad mood now. She wanted her husband to retire as much as he did, and had for years, but he felt he couldn't just jump ship. Someone had to run the place, so he was forced to, against his will. Spencer and Marcy agreed that he was hurting the store, but he refused to listen, and made a series of poor investments, which hurt the business even more.

Spencer consulted Barton White, an investment advisor the family had used before, to discuss their stock portfolio. He was young and solid, and extremely bright, had gone to Yale, and had the same concerns she did about her father's risky investments, switching from stocks to commodities. Since it was a family-owned business, there was no one to stop him. Tucker was the CEO now, in full control. Thornton had never trusted Tucker to make investments on his own, and some of his financial decisions were frankly alarming. Thornton had always kept a firm grip on the reins and the purse strings and now Tucker had control of both. He enjoyed the power more than he loved the store, unlike his father. The store had been a living, breathing being to Thornton, but not to his son.

Barton White invited Spencer out to dinner in the course of discussing their stock portfolio. And needing someone knowledgeable, objective, intelligent, and sane to talk to, she gratefully accepted. Without her grandfather, she had no one to talk to anymore, or advise her, or whom she trusted, other than Marcy, who understood fashion, not finance.

Bart was extremely conservative in all things, which was reassuring from an investment standpoint, and made him less interesting as a date. Until then, she had mostly dated men she'd met in college and graduate school. Bart was more of an adult, although only six years older than she was. He was solid and stable though not exciting. Spencer had had a disappointing romance in college that had soured her on long-term commitments. Her greatest commitment was to the store. She felt so lost without her grandfather's good advice that she got more deeply involved with Bart faster than she might have otherwise. She felt vulnerable and alone. She was constantly at odds with her father, and her wonderful grandfather was gone. He was so much to lose and left a terrible void in her life.

Spencer felt wide open and even scared some of the time, which was unlike her. It speeded up her relationship with Bart dramatically, and she clung to him and relied on him.

Spencer got close to Bart at a moment of fear, need, and isolation in her life. Her father took full advantage of his new position as CEO with no one to control him, and every conversation Spencer had with him led to an argument. He finally had the freedom he wanted, although he hated his job and resented the store. He refused to listen to reason, and Bart assured Spencer that her theories and concerns were sound. He validated what she thought.

Bart was startled and impressed by how bright she was, and how mature for her age. She was cautious in her decisions, and the knowledge she'd acquired from her grandfather served her well. Bart wasn't used to dealing with women as capable as Spencer, particularly not at her age.

She'd been groomed to run a business with expert skill. It attracted him to her, and was a new experience for him. His own mother had never worked, was on numerous charity committees, and had no interest in the business world. None of the girls he had dated had serious jobs, or even worked. They were debutantes and went to parties and didn't challenge him mentally. Pretty and fun to be with had always been enough for him. Spencer was so much more. She had a great head for business, and was still feminine at the same time. He could talk to her about his own job, and hers as well, and he liked advising her about her father's constant mistakes, which she spotted every time.

Bart advised her to find someone to hire that she could groom to be CEO eventually. Sooner or later, her father would retire, and she'd need someone to run the store for her, so she could lead a life of her own. She laughed at that idea.

"That someone is me, Bart. The store **is** my life." He never realized to what degree she meant it and didn't believe her at the time.

"You say that now. You won't want to do this forever. One day you'll want to be married and have kids." She never shared with him her profound belief that you could do both, have a family **and** run a business. She was sure that she could do it, but was afraid to say it to Bart, for fear he'd think her unfeminine or tough. But one day she hoped to have a husband and children, and still run the store.

After watching her father mismanage it, she had no desire to turn it over to someone else one day when her father finally did retire. She did every-thing she could to learn all she'd need to know later on. She was quiet and methodical, and Bart had no idea how serious she was. He thought that running the store was just a time-passer for her before mar-riage and that she never considered it a long-term career.

Spencer was startled when six months after they started dating, Bart proposed. She enjoyed being with him, had come to love him for all the support and advice he gave her. She had been relying on him, and he seemed like the ideal husband because he was so solid and knew so much about her busi-ness. He wasn't as fun-loving as some of the men she'd dated, but he seemed like the right long-term partner for life. It was a decision she made seriously, and they got engaged.

They married after a six-month engagement, a year after they'd started dating. It was long enough to plan a wedding, and she found a beautiful wed-ding dress and Marcy ordered it through the store. They wanted children, but Spencer planned to wait for several years. She felt too young and didn't want children until the store was solid again, until after the damage her father had done could be corrected. She assumed that Bart agreed, although they never discussed it in detail.

One of the things she and Bart had in common was how similar their parents were. Neither of their mothers had ever worked or had any interest in business or their husband's jobs. They preferred more frivolous, feminine pursuits. Both sets of parents were extremely conservative and had old-fashioned ideas, which didn't seem to bother Bart, although Spencer's parents were a constant source of annoyance to her. Bart was more tolerant of his, and agreed with them more than Spencer realized. She never fully understood how deeply conservative he was too, much more so than she. Her grandfather had encouraged her to be forward-thinking, innovative, and modern. Bart had no similar influence in his life and was more traditional than he admitted. He didn't want to seem stuffy to her. And she didn't want to appear too brash and bold to him.

The first big shock in their marriage hit them hard and fast, shortly after their honeymoon, which they spent skiing in Aspen. Spencer caught a cold that turned rapidly into bronchitis, and a local doctor prescribed an antibiotic, which helped quickly but caused her birth control to fail. Weeks after their honeymoon, she discovered that she was pregnant.

Spencer was in shock. The baby she wanted in several years, not months, was on its way. Bart loved the idea, and Spencer was stunned, and even more so when they learned that it was twins. For the first time, Bart told her clearly that he expected her to give up work when the babies were born. He wanted the kind of mother for his children that he'd had, one who stayed at home, not one who ran a store. The battles began then. Spencer refused to quit her job, and worked for the entire pregnancy, until two weeks before the twins were born. There was a raging battle between Spencer and Bart for nine months. She refused to abandon her grandfather's store and didn't see why she should. Bart's parents were in full agreement with him and disapproved of her. Her own mother sided with them. Spencer felt constantly guilty but stuck to her beliefs and stubbornly refused to quit her job. It was a chronic source of arguments between her and Bart.

She gave birth to identical twin boys ten months after she and Bart were married. They named them Ben and Axel. They weighed five pounds each. And due to the rapid pregnancy, the shock of having twins, the pressures of her job, constant battles with her father, worrying about the store and the way her father was running it, and fights with Bart about not quitting her job, the marriage started to lose altitude almost as soon as it got off the ground.

They spent their entire first year and their first anniversary arguing, with Spencer in tears when Bart told her he thought they should sell the store. Her job was too much for her, he said, and he felt it was incompatible with marriage and trying to raise twins. Her father hated his job and it was only a matter of time before he would retire, and Bart didn't want her to run the store. He wanted her at home with their boys. Tucker agreed with Bart that they should sell.

"I'm not going to sell the store just because we had twins," she said to Bart, outraged. "That's ridiculous." Feeling guilty, she had gone back to work eight weeks after the boys were born. She and Bart had hired a competent baby nurse who was experienced with twins.

"It's more ridiculous that you went back to work after eight weeks, and you stopped nursing them." He had child-rearing ideas she didn't agree with, since his mother had never worked, and had taken care of him and his brother herself without a nanny. Spencer had grown up with a housekeeper who took care of her. She had spent more time with her than with her mother, although her mother didn't work, but went to lunch a lot and played bridge with friends. "What **are** your priorities?" Bart asked

Spencer angrily. He seemed to disapprove of everything she did and criticized her constantly. She already felt guilty enough leaving her babies to go back to work, but she had a responsibility to the store too. She was determined to manage both roles successfully.

"My priorities are the same as they were before. You, now our babies, and the store," she said heatedly. She'd made no secret of it.

"You can't do it all. You have to pick a lane," he said angrily. "You can't be a mother and work."

"Yes, I can. I can do all three, work, and be a wife and mother." She sincerely believed that and was trying her best. It was hard at times, but there was room in her heart for all of it.

"It doesn't look like it to me. You come home at eight o'clock every night. And when was the last time we went to dinner or a movie together?" he asked her. He had a point. She felt even guiltier when he said it. She came home exhausted every night from everything she did at work. She kept an eye on everything and was diligent about her job. And she wanted to be a good wife and mother too.

"We're still adjusting to the twins," she said defensively. And Bart was adjusting to Francine, the nanny, and hated having someone living in the house with them. But without the nanny, Spencer would have had to be up all night feeding and changing the babies. This way, at least she got some sleep, so she could function at the office.

"This isn't going to work unless you change something, Spencer," Bart warned her. "And your father is going to run the place into the ground before you can get your hands on the controls. You might as well sell it now, while you can still get top dollar for it."

It broke her heart to hear him say that. She didn't want a war with him, or an ultimatum, telling her to quit her job and sell the store, and she could see that he was working up to it. In a way, Bart was jealous of the store, and always had been, because it meant so much to her, and she didn't try to hide it. She had explained it to him as soon as they started dating, and he had claimed he didn't mind. But now that they were married and had two babies, he had changed his tune and wanted her to get rid of the store and was trying to convince her father too. It was a choice she didn't want to have to make, for him or anyone else. She was convinced she could do it all. It became his battle cry every time they had a fight, which was an increasingly frequent oc-currence. Then the bottom dropped out of her world again.

When the twins were four months old, her fa-ther was diagnosed with pancreatic cancer. He died in three months. It was a rapid descent into hell, and a merciful end when it came quickly. She barely had time to adjust and take over. But once she did, she was surprised how comfortable she was running the store. She loved it and remembered everything her grandfather had taught her. It was as though she could hear his voice in her head every day, telling her what to do in each situation. With Marcy Parker's help, she reinstated most of the lines her father had eliminated, and the increase in sales was almost immediate. By the time her father died, she was in full control of the store.

Her mother, Eileen, blamed the store for Tucker's death at only seventy, so much younger than his own parents. He had run it for only four years, as a duty he hated every single day. Eileen had always wished she had married a banker, or a man involved in finance like her own father. Spencer had begun to realize that she herself had married one of "them," someone like her parents, not someone like her grandfather, or like her. It was a thrill for her every time the store did well, or some marketing plan or special merchandising had borne fruit. She loved seeing the people shopping in the store, excited by what they'd found, and leaving the store with smiles on their faces. Thornton had taken pleasure in that too. He genuinely loved what he did. It wasn't just a moneymaking machine to him, it was a way of helping people find real pleasure in what they bought, whether it was a woman with a new bracelet from the jewelry department, or a new hat, or a man with a cashmere or alpaca topcoat from the best tailor in London, or a pair of exquisitely made riding boots.

Spencer had initiated a new department with Marcy Parker, consisting of some lovely items at more affordable prices, and it had done extremely well, attracting a slightly broader range of customer, many of them young and on smaller budgets than their parents. Spencer and Marcy took real pleasure in offering them quality goods too, at lower prices. The department was a huge success. Marcy was a smart, lively, energetic, chic woman, long divorced with no children, who was a hundred percent dedicated to the store, and a good friend to Spencer.

Brooke's still had the millinery department Hannabel had inspired in the beginning, and a counter where customers could order custom-made gloves from France. The store was a treasure trove of beautiful items which gave people a thrill to own. There was no way Spencer could give that up. It was a labor of love, not just a job.

At the same time, she wanted to be a good wife to Bart, and a good mother to Ben and Axel. She knew she had much to learn about motherhood and it was all new to her, but when she held the twins in her arms, she felt a surge of something she had never felt before, a bond like no other. She wanted to protect them with every ounce of her being.

She knew that other women worked and managed to combine it successfully with motherhood. Women who were doctors, lawyers, nurses, artists, people with jobs and careers they cared about, and they loved their children. What was so wrong about her nurturing the family business that her grandfather had put so much love into, and being a mother too? Why did it have to be a choice between one path or the other? It seemed so unfair to her for Bart to force the issue. She knew she couldn't sell the business just to please him. She would have resented him forever if she did. She wanted a chance to learn to do both things well, mothering, and running the store now that it was hers at last.

No matter how hard she tried to explain it to him, Bart refused to understand how she felt. Her father's death caused increased tension between them, as she spent longer and longer hours at the store, with the changes she made after Tucker's death. Their nanny, Francine, tried to keep the babies up until she came home, which wasn't always possible, but she juggled their feeding schedule so that on most nights it was. And Spencer didn't mind keeping them up later so she could see them. It was pure joy for her when she came home and held them in her arms.

Bart spent no more time with them than Spencer did, in fact, considerably less, which he felt was fine for him. He said that it was more her job than his, to be a constant presence with their babies as infants, and throughout their childhood. They were seven months old when their grandfather died, but he had taken little interest in them, and their grandmother Eileen was a rare visitor too, even after she was widowed. She played more bridge with her friends and was too depressed for several months to make time to see the twins. In fact, despite how hard she worked, Spencer was the only family member who engaged with the twins. Bart's parents weren't attentive either.

Spencer tried to be available to her mother, and felt sorry for her, but they were no more compatible after her father's death than they had been before. Her parents had always been closer to each other than they had been to her. She had always felt like an intruder. Their uncertainty about wanting children had persisted even after she was born, and Spencer had always felt how tentative her parents were about her, unlike her grandparents, who welcomed her into their lives, even after her grandfather's initial disappointment that she wasn't a boy. Thornton had set a standard of excellence for her that she had never failed to meet. She had never disappointed him, and he recognized early on, and had been willing to admit, that she was as smart as any man. Tucker had been far less willing to acknowledge his daughter's accomplishments and was far more old-fashioned and chauvinistic than his father, who recognized the competence of the women who worked for him, and rewarded them accordingly, as he had Marcy Parker, who had one of the highest-paying jobs in the store.

It was daunting at first for Spencer to take over as CEO at thirty. Then she remembered that her grandfather had been exactly her age when he first opened his store. But it had been much smaller then. Spencer had a sizable operation on her hands, and all the responsibilities that went with it. There were articles about her in the business section of **The New York Times,** and another in **The Wall Street Journal.** She was one of the youngest CEOs in New York. The reporters traced the history of the store, and made due note of the changes she had made, interweaving them with the traditions she had kept in their current model. The one person who offered no praise or support was her husband. It was hard to understand, but Bart seemed even more angry and jealous the moment she took over the store, once her father was dying and too ill to work.

She didn't admit it, but it was almost a relief when she didn't have to fight her father anymore, and she could run the store as she knew her grandfather would have. She promoted Marcy Parker to president almost immediately, instead of just fashion director, and brought in a new fashion director she hired away from Neiman Marcus in Dallas. It angered some people that she hadn't filled the position internally, but she thought some new blood and a fresh eye would be good for the store, and she was right.

The new fashion director was an elegant Texan named Beauregard Vincent. He had spent ten years working for Christian Dior in Paris, and four at Neiman Marcus. He was thirty-nine years old, and his credentials were impeccable. Miraculously, he and Marcy got along. She was fifty-five years old, born and raised in New York, and had a few sharp edges. She had worked her way up through the ranks and had a great eye for fashion and an instinct for new trends. She was loyal to Spencer, as she had been to her grandfather. Beau's point of view was more traditional, very influenced by high-end French brands. They balanced each other well. Spencer was pleased with her new hire, and said as much to Bart, but despite his own skills in business, he had no interest in the store. He was adamant about wanting her to sell it. Nothing she did or said changed his mind.

"I'm not going to sell," Spencer finally said to Bart six months after her father died. The twins had turned one a month before, and she had just turned thirty-one, was hitting her stride as CEO, and felt comfortable in her new role. She was managing both motherhood and her job, and proving that she could do both well, which Bart refused to admit. He continued to criticize her constantly and made her feel guilty whenever he could.

"You'll wish you had sold," Bart said, "when your father's bad investments tank and come home to roost. You'll start losing money, and wish you'd gotten rid of the business when you could." He predicted defeat at every turn, and never success. It was demoralizing, which was his intention. "I could see your working there when your grandfather was alive, and even to support your father, but running the store now is a whole other statement," he said. "It makes you look power-hungry and tough." He never had a kind word to say about the job she was doing or acknowledged how hard it was at times. His own job on Wall Street was demanding but not exciting, and not as big a job as hers. He was an anonymous investment advisor in a large investment firm. He had none of the glory and attention she was getting as a young and promising CEO. He was angry at Spencer all the time, jealous of everything she did.

"I'm the fourth generation in a family business, Bart. Why does that bug you so much?" She was kind and loving to him. And he never had a decent word to say to her.

"I wanted a wife and a mother for my children, not a CEO. It's like being married to a man." Some of the things he said cut her to the quick, and she tried not to let it show. She didn't crow to him about her successes, so as not to bruise his ego, but she didn't want to be beaten down by him either. It was all he did now.

"I'm not going to sell," she reiterated, holding firm. "What do you want to do about it?" she said to him softly one morning over breakfast. She kept hoping he would adjust to her new position. She tried to make it as unobtrusive for him as possible, but it was what it was. And she was doing a good job.

"I want you to sell the store, if you want to save our marriage," he said bluntly, and she looked shocked. He had never put it quite that clearly.

"Are you telling me you'll divorce me if I don't sell the store?" she asked, looking him directly in the eyes. She didn't like the anger and jealousy she saw there, and she was tired of it.

"I guess I am," he said coldly. "It's only going to get worse between us if you keep the store." Their sex life had dwindled to nothing once she became

CEO. It was as though the very idea emasculated him and he no longer found her attractive. If anything, he found the whole idea repellent. She didn't want to force herself on him, and although she was young and beautiful, he never wanted to make love to her anymore. He never told her she was pretty or acted like he noticed it.

"You're not giving me much choice," she said with a chill in her voice. Something in her had finally snapped.

"Yes, I am. You can sell the store if you want this marriage. Or you can keep the store and lose me." For the first time, she wondered if he was cheating on her. But in the weeks after he said it to her, she realized that even if she sold the store, it wouldn't save their marriage. He was too bitter now, and too competitive with her. Every day was a contest as to who was the most successful. They both knew she was, and he would never forgive her for it. He did well at his job, but it was just a job, and for Spencer the store was a lifelong passion, and a legacy from her grandfather. Nothing could induce her to give that up, or to betray her grandfather's memory by selling the store. And she wanted to keep it now for her sons.

She conceded defeat a month later, after thinking it over seriously. There was nothing left to salvage. Bart had lost all goodwill toward her, and compassion for her, and even physical attraction to her. He just saw her as some kind of robot or mannequin wearing what she brought home from the store. He didn't see her as beautiful anymore, and she could feel it. He was too jealous of her to love her. It was obvious he no longer did, if he ever had. She doubted it now. But whatever he had felt for her was gone. It was chilling to be around him. Everything that had originally attracted him to her, her energy, her entrepreneurial skills, her brain, were what he resented and made him appear to hate her now. She felt detested by him most of the time. And he treated her with anger, disrespect, and disdain, to punish her for her success.

The idea of bringing up the twins alone was daunting. But being married to a man who resented her every hour of every day wasn't appealing either. In the end, it was Spencer who filed the divorce. By the time she did, she had accepted the demise of their two-year marriage as unavoidable, and maybe even predictable, although she hadn't seen it in the beginning. He wanted to control her and deprive her of the store. It was different in the beginning. He had actually seemed as though he admired and respected her. Now it was clear he no longer did. She wasn't what he expected of a wife and mother. The ground rules had changed once she had the twins.

The attorney she went to filed all the papers for her and sent them to Bart's attorney. There was no set visitation schedule for the twins, since they were too young for regular visitation, and she stipulated that with advance warning, Bart could visit them at her home whenever he wanted. He had moved out temporarily and was staying at his club, since Spencer had bought the apartment where they lived. She had had the funds to buy it, Bart hadn't.

Bart's attorney asked for the apartment as part of the settlement, and she gave it to him. She bought a small townhouse in Chelsea, not far from the store, and decorated it the way she wanted. She loved it. It was just big enough for her and the twins, with a room for the nanny, and a garden. The twins seemed happy there too.

She was working even harder than before, once she and Bart split up, and rushing home to see the twins after work. She felt like a robot sometimes, going from one problem to the next. She was the only parent at home, and the ultimate decision-maker and the final word at the store on every subject. It was an awesome responsibility, and she took it more seriously than ever. She took her parenting of the twins seriously too, and managed both her career and her mothering, just as she had promised herself she would. She was surprised by how little Bart wanted to see the boys. She invited him to visit them whenever he hadn't been to see them in a while, and most of the time he said he was busy and declined. He hadn't formed a strong bond with them to begin with, and it seemed to lessen over time. He was enjoying his single life again, and dating. Spencer had no time to date, between the store and the twins, and she had no interest in dating. She didn't have the energy or the time to meet men and go out with them.

Her mother had been very vocally opposed to the divorce as soon as Spencer told her. As usual, she was critical of Spencer. Her views were more similar to Bart's than her daughter's. And like Bart, she hated the store, and was jealous of it.

"He's right, you know. You don't have time to bring up children properly. They'll end up juvenile delinquents if you're never around," she predicted. Eileen had never been around either, and Spencer had never gone wild. She'd been a serious child and a good student, despite little attention from her parents. Spencer was a much better, warmer mother than her own had been, and spent more time with her children than her mother had.

"I'm around, Mom," Spencer said quietly. "Just not at traditional hours." She took care of them herself on Sundays and loved it. She didn't have to choose between them and the store. It was Bart who had tried to force that hand, as though to prove a point. He was giving her a decent amount of child support for the boys, but none of his time. She wondered who he was dating, but never asked. She told herself that it was none of her business, although it would be later on, once visitation started. The court mediator had started visitation at three years of age for the twins, by mutual consent, with visits at Spencer's home in the meantime, with proper warning. Bart almost never called to see them. He claimed they were too young to know the difference. The twins seemed happy, had no alarming behaviors, and didn't seem to miss him. They were only eighteen months old, barely more than babies, and had been just over a year old when their parents separated.

Spencer walked the store, as she did every morning right after they opened at ten, although she was there long before ten. She was thirty-seven years old, had run the store for seven years since her father's death, and her divorce from Bart had been final for five years. It had been relatively bloodless. They'd had a strong prenup at her father's insistence, and as a result there had been less to argue about than there might have been, once she gave him their apartment, which was generous of her. In the end, neither of them tried to hang onto a marriage that wasn't working and never would. He had disappeared from her life rapidly, which was a relief. He said he wanted a traditional wife who stayed home, not one with a big job who owned a department store and was a CEO. He had wanted her to quit her job at the store once she had children. He refused to understand how much the store meant to her. She had a deep love for it at the very core of her being, and considered it an important part of her heritage and her history. It was almost sacred to her, and a mission bequeathed to her by her grandfather.

Bart still didn't see the boys often enough, in her opinion, but they weren't suffering. She had fun with them on Sundays, when Francine was off, and she tried to get home several times a week to have dinner with them, or at least tuck them into bed. And she saw them every morning before work. Francine, the nanny, had stayed with them, so she was a constant.

Bart had been seeing the same woman for the past year, as the boys reported to her after the rare times when they saw him for dinner or a brief visit. He never had them spend the night and didn't want to. He said they were too hard to manage and too exuberant. He still couldn't tell them apart, and didn't try. She expected him to get married again at some point.

She currently had an off-and-on dating relationship with Bill Kelly, the account executive at the ad
agency she used for the store. Bill was forty years
old, had never been married, and enjoyed his freedom. The relationship was more of a convenience
for both of them than a serious romance, and company when it suited them both. Neither of them
wanted to get married or made strong demands on
each other. They were both busy. Spencer had her
hands and her life full with the store and the twins.
For now, she didn't need or want more than occasional companionship. Her marriage to Bart hadn't
inspired her to want to try again. The marriage had
been a major disappointment. She was afraid now
that any man she got seriously involved with would
have issues about her dedication to her job. Her
boys and the store were more important to her than
any man she had met so far.

She smiled as she went from floor to floor on the
escalator, casting a quick eye into each department,
just to make sure that all was going smoothly and so
that the store personnel would see her. It was a good
reminder to them that she was a hands-on CEO,
and that customer service was very important to
her. She wanted every customer happy while they
were there and delighted with their purchases when
they left. Walking the store every morning was

something she had learned from her grandfather. He had warned her not to get tied up in her office and forget to show her face every day to the staff and the customers. She had often walked with him on his morning rounds.

She had grown into her role in the past seven years, although Thornton's shoes were hard to fill. But eleven years after his death, she was still trying, and hoped he would have been proud of her. Her father's tenure had been brief, and of no benefit to the store. It was Spencer who added her own vitality and love to it.

When she reached the ground floor, she took the elevator back up to her office. She walked past her secretary in the reception area with a smile, closed her office door, and sat down at her grandfather's desk. She could almost feel him smiling at her, as she started her day in earnest. She had lots to do today. She always did, and liked it that way.

She loved being busy, and feeling as though she had accomplished something at the end of every day when she went home to the twins. The store met her needs almost like a human being. It had a heart and a soul, which had been infused into it by the people who loved it. It was her turn to nurture it now, protect it and help it grow, until one day one or both of her sons would be old enough to run it, and she would pass the torch to them. Until then, it was her mission, and she rose to the challenge every day. She could see herself growing old there, as her grandfather had. And someday it would be her legacy to Axel and Ben. It was the best gift she could give them, just as it had been the greatest gift her grandfather left her, when she inherited the store from her father. She could already imagine changing the name of the store one day to add Axel and Ben's name to hers, "Brooke and White." But for now, until they grew up, the magical world of Brooke's was hers.

Chapter 2

Mike Weston was a man who moved quickly and made rapid decisions, good ones most of the time. Harvard-educated, he was the son of hardworking middle-class parents. His father, Max, had made a fortune from managing his money well, building small businesses into big ones and selling them at an enormous profit. Max had an entrepreneurial spirit and an unfailing eye for moneymaking opportunities with simple ideas that others overlooked. He had made his first fortune buying lots in bad neighborhoods and turning them into parking lots and later garages. He sold them at a high price when the neighborhoods became gentrified. He had bought into the fast-food industry early on, franchise by franchise, and made a fortune on that. Mike's mother, Beverly, had gotten involved in the internet shopping craze, with appealing, low-priced goods. With her husband's help and sound advice, she had turned her business into a mammoth venture with minimal overhead and maximum profit, and was among the pioneers of the business. Now there were trucks with her name on them in every major city, and her own fortune rivaled her husband's. Mike's sister, Stephanie, worked for her.

Mike came by his knack for picking great opportunities with a Midas touch. He loved talking business with his father, he always learned something from him. Max had never gone to college, but he was brilliant at making money, and so was Mike. Mike didn't build businesses from scratch the way his father did. He invested in them, in widely diversified fields. He invested in high-tech, the pharmaceutical industry, large real estate developments, minerals, and oil. He had learned something about fashion from his mother and had done very well buying low-priced brands and multiplying their volume of sales exponentially before he sold them or took them public. He had a nose for great deals and was highly respected for his successful ventures. He had a group of solid investors desperate to get in on his deals.

By the time he was thirty-four Mike had made

his own fortune, which was even greater than his father's. He was more willing to take risks, within reason, and chase industries he studied carefully, and so far he had never gone wrong. Ten years after he had won his reputation as the golden boy of the investment world, his corporate involvements were as diversified as his interests. At forty-four, he was still moving at lightning speed and on the rise. And along with his brilliance, he was a strikingly handsome man. He appeared to have it all. He made a fortune for his investors and himself.

Mike wasn't some crazy wild man jumping off a cliff. He calculated everything he did with infinite precision, assessed the risks, and then took the leap, which was why the investors who followed him trusted him implicitly. They'd ridden the internet wave early, at the right time, and he'd played with some fun investments too, but only if they made sense financially. He had made astonishingly few mistakes. He was relentless to deal with, and honorable. His competitors and his allies respected him, even though they said he was tough. But he had to be, so he didn't let his investors down. He hated to have anyone lose money on a deal.

He wasn't the young golden boy of Wall Street anymore. He had grown up, and he was said to be brilliant and an honest man. Time had flown while he was working hard, always chasing deals, and he couldn't believe how old his kids were now. His daughter, Jennifer, was nineteen and a sophomore at Stanford. She wanted to go to law school after she graduated. His son Zack's strong suit was science, and Mike thought he should go to MIT, but eighteen-year-old Zack had decided to take a gap year instead after high school. He had been trekking through Europe for six months. He'd been in Turkey, Italy, Spain, Poland, and Germany, and was currently in France. Mike was eager for him to get back into school, but Zack didn't have his sister's ambition or his father's. He was a gentler, less driven person. It was the one thing Mike and his son disagreed on. He didn't want Zack to get lost in the woods. He needed a direction, a trajectory he hadn't found yet, and a burst of energy to go with it. Mike wasn't sure that discovering the wonders of French wine, the churches in Italy, and the beauty of the wild horses in Camargue were going to be part of a career path for him. He was a sweet boy with a warm heart, searching for a sign from the universe about what direction to go. Mike hoped he'd find it soon. He worried about Zack a lot and couldn't wait for him to come home. He missed him terribly.

It was one of Mike's many disagreements with his wife, Maureen. She thought Mike pressured Zack too much to find a career path. Maureen was the keeper of Mike's long list of past sins, and there were many according to her, most of them related to his career and success, which she listed among his crimes, more specifically that he worked all the time and never came home except to sleep, spending more time on his deals than with his wife and kids, which he conceded was not entirely untrue. But he would never have achieved all that he had if he'd been around more. You didn't craft a success like his by going to Cub Scout meetings, ballet recitals, and cocktail parties with your wife, which were all low priorities to him, and always had been. But then one day, the kids grew up and left and you'd missed the boat. He was well aware of that now. He had regrets about it and he loved them, but he couldn't turn back the clock. Jennifer understood, was all forgiving of her father, and had the same drive he did. Zack was out in the stratosphere, and had his own priorities and style, very different from his father's, but Zack was tolerant about him, and wasn't angry at what they'd missed. Both of his children understood that he'd been building an empire and a safety net for them while he was busy. Maureen didn't, and gave him no free passes.

Zack was still a little lost, which Maureen claimed would not have been the case if Mike had been around more. Now Zack was eighteen and had no idea what to do next. Maureen blamed his father, as she did for almost everything. She painted Mike as a bad guy, even to his kids, which didn't seem fair to Mike. She was seething with anger at him, for all the things he hadn't done for twenty years. They'd been in a bad space for the last three or four. Mike had lost count, but it seemed like a long time. He had gotten used to the tension between them and hadn't noticed precisely when it slipped from occasional to their normal state. She was angry all the time now, whenever he came home.

They had drifted apart even further since the kids had been gone, Zack to Europe for the last six months, and Jennifer to Stanford the year before. Ever since the kids left, Maureen had dropped the pretense that she even liked him. As a result, Mike had given up and they had stopped making any effort with each other. She was always burning with anger about something. With the kids gone, they no longer had to pretend that they got along. Their animosity was a poorly kept secret anyway, and Mike was sure it was part of why Zack had taken a year off and left. He couldn't stand the tension at home anymore. Mike was used to it, and he was away a lot for work. And Maureen's constant sarcastic remarks and complaints no longer hit their mark nor wounded him as deeply. Most of her complaints were ancient history, since the kids were gone, but she complained anyway. It had been the language of their relationship for years. She claimed that he expected too much of the kids and said that not everyone was as driven as he was or wanted to be. He believed in hard work.

Mike could no longer pinpoint when things had started to go wrong in their marriage. It happened when he wasn't looking, making deals somewhere, taking one of his companies public and on the road for the IPO, or rounding up investors. There had been years when he'd hardly been home. He readily admitted it now. He'd been building a future for them. Maureen wasn't wrong about his being away too much, and somewhere along the way, she had become bitter and had given up. She resented him with every fiber of her being now. It came through her pores like venom.

It had all been so promising when they started out. She was from San Francisco, the daughter of a major venture capitalist, so a busy, ambitious father was familiar to her. She was the junior assistant to a junior editor at a fashion magazine in New York, young and beautiful, and he was in business school at Columbia. She'd gone to college at NYU for two years and decided to stay and play. Mike was dazzling when she met him, and her father had approved of the match as soon as he spoke to him, when Maureen brought Mike home for a weekend in San Francisco. He liked Mike's drive and energy and ambition, and thought he'd be a great husband. He was a serious, hardworking young man with impressive goals. Maureen had loved Mike's good looks and ignored the rest. He hadn't hidden his career plans from her. She just didn't listen, pay attention, or believe him. He had become exactly what he said he would, a big financial success like his own father, and hers. And then she came to resent him and hate him for it because he worked hard and was always busy. He loved their children but spent too little time with them. He saw that now and regretted it. She wouldn't forgive him. She was relentless in her listing of his failures and remembered them all. It was hard to live with, being constantly reminded of the countless times he had disappointed her. When she met him, she could tell in the first five minutes that Mike Weston was going places and would go far. It was in his style and in his pores. He never hid how ambitious he was, or the dreams he intended to pursue. Her father, Allan Stanton, knew immediately that if Maureen married him, his daughter would be in good hands. And he wasn't wrong. Mike was responsible and as passionate about her, and as attentive, as he was about starting his career. And then somehow, when he finished business school, his career took over. He was young and handsome and exciting. She was fun and easy to be with, much brighter than her job required. She didn't have any great interests or ambitions, and had grown up protected and materially spoiled by her parents. She wasn't after money. She had her own in trust from her grandparents, and was used to the finer things in life.

Mike thought she was the most beautiful girl he'd ever seen when he met her. Now, twenty years later, at forty-two, she was still beautiful, but the light had gone out in her eyes. Mike was just as handsome and exciting at forty-four as he had been twenty years before, success had only enhanced him. But he looked at her differently now. They both knew it, but neither of them had noticed when the fire had gone out, while she was complaining.

Maureen had inherited a vast fortune when her father died five years into their marriage. She had never had another job after she and Mike were married. She never got involved in any major projects or philanthropic causes. She had concentrated on their two children, and was a devoted mother, but both children were gone now. And she had no reason to get a job. She didn't need or want one. She was waiting for Zack to come home from Europe.

Mike had moved into the guest room as soon as Zack left, and moved back to his and Maureen's bedroom when the kids came home for the holidays. Sleeping in separate rooms was just easier and gave Mike and Maureen both space from each other, which was a relief. He planned to move back in again when the kids came home. But in the meantime, it gave him and Maureen room to breathe. She sucked the air out of him with her constant reproaches and recriminations.

She liked to read late at night, and he was an early riser. But once the kids were gone, he realized that they were strangers living under one roof. She never failed to remind him that he had sacrificed her and their children for his career. He was never going to be able to make up for it, and it was easier not having to listen to it every night.

He stayed late at the office most nights. They went to social events together occasionally to keep up appearances publicly, but less and less frequently. Being together was painful. Maureen was used to telling people he was out of town on business or working late. No one was surprised to see her alone, and she didn't seem to mind it. People sometimes wondered if they were still together, but no one dared ask. Mike told himself they had stayed together for the children. But he wondered if it was true. Jennifer and Zack weren't babies anymore. They would have adjusted if their parents divorced. But Mike and Maureen were used to each other.

They knew who they were dealing with and where the bodies were buried. It seemed infinitely simpler to stay together than to cause a major upheaval and start a new life. Mike never thought about leaving her, and contented himself with what they had. She was a good mother to their children, and they had intelligent conversations when she wasn't angry at him. She was a bright woman even though she had done nothing with her intelligence. He wondered if things would have been different if she had. Unwinding twenty years now would be difficult, and there was never a good time to do it. So, he stayed late at the office, and she was still asleep when he left for work. After sleeping in the guest room, as he had for months, he hardly felt married to her. That had been a big change, but she never even commented on it. Having separate bedrooms suited her too, although they never admitted it to each other.

When he came home at night, she was often out with friends. She had a circle of people she went to parties and the theater with. He went to business dinners without her. They led parallel lives, which intersected as seldom as they could arrange.

He missed the children now that they were away. It had come much faster than he expected. Maureen had warned him of that, and he hadn't listened. He called Jennifer in California two or three times a week. Zack was harder to reach, floating around Europe, and half the time he forgot to buy a SIM card when he moved to a new location and his family couldn't call him. He had come home for Christmas for two weeks and gone back to Europe with his two friends who were taking a gap year with him. They were good boys and didn't get in trouble, but Mike wanted Zack to be in college and get an education. This wasn't Mike's dream for him, but for now, everything was on hold. The three friends were having a good time and Zack didn't seem eager for it to be over, and who could blame him. Floating around Europe for a year sounded good to Mike too. It was something he had never done. His father would never have let him. In his youth, with his parents, you either went to school or you worked. You didn't drift around Europe with a Eurail Pass and a backpack. Mike's parents were shocked that he'd let Zack do it, but Maureen had been a strong influence, and fully approved of Zack having fun for a year before starting college. She didn't want him becoming driven like his father. Jennifer was already so much like him, Maureen didn't want their son to be too, sacrificing his home life and family for a career. She thought it was the worst lesson Mike had taught them. Her own father had been like that, and Mike's parents were too. Mike's father was nearly seventy and still building his empire because he enjoyed it. His mother was running her mammoth business at sixty-seven. Maureen had nothing in common with any of them, not even Mike. And her mother had been like her, never engaged in anything, and she had died relatively young, having never done anything except indulging herself and spending money, and her husband never objected.

Maureen had friends she enjoyed, some of whom Mike didn't even know, and she didn't introduce him. She had had an absentee husband for most of their marriage. It was just the way things had worked out. They let it happen. She didn't ask herself the difficult questions, like if she still loved him. It didn't make any difference now, and she didn't want to know the answers. And by now, neither did he. It was best not to think about it.

Mike started his morning meeting at nine o'clock sharp every day, to bring his close associates up to speed on the projects they were working on, the new investments they were considering, and work in progress on various deals. He arrived at the office at eight A.M. himself. He liked a quiet hour to gather his thoughts and get organized. He was up at six every day and read **The New York Times** and **The Wall Street Journal** before he came to work.

He read the London **Financial Times** on the weekends. With the children gone, he had more time on the weekends, no basketball games to attend for Zack, or parties to drive Jenny to or pick her up from at midnight. He had made more of an attempt to be attentive to them in their final high school years, but it was late in the day, and whatever he did was never enough to satisfy Maureen, and even if the kids didn't complain, she always did. The kids were close to their father when they saw him and didn't object to his busy work life and frequent trips. They were proud of what he'd accomplished. Maureen wasn't.

Now he had more free time to play tennis and golf on the weekends, usually with business associates, or important investors he was courting. Almost everything he did related to business somehow. Maureen considered that a cardinal sin too.

They had a house in the country that they seldom used now, with the kids gone, and hadn't for several years. The kids' weekend activities kept them in town, and he didn't want to get trapped in the country alone with Maureen. Their house in Connecticut stood empty all the time now, and he didn't miss it. Maureen had moved there in the summer for a month or two, while he stayed in the city to work. They went to Maine for three weeks every summer with the kids, to sail and have barbecues. Jenny had taken a summer job in San Francisco for the coming summer, so the trip to Maine was uncertain this year, unless Zack came home and wanted to go. This was a whole new chapter in Mike and Maureen's lives. They couldn't count on their children to distract them and keep them together.

Mike's investment team walked into his office promptly at nine. His office was sleek and modern, with chrome and glass, a long wooden desk, and contemporary art on the walls. It wasn't cozy, but it was elegant and efficient, on the forty-seventh floor with a breathtaking view of New York.

Will Stinson was the senior member of the team. He was their specialist in bio and high-tech investments. Joe Weiss knew more about real estate development than anyone Mike had ever hired, and Renee Durant was a fantastic research source for what Mike called the "softer" brands, unusual investments that had done well for the firm. She had suggested the low-priced women's fashion brand that had proven to be brilliantly lucrative, although Mike's mother had turned her nose up when he asked her about it. But it had become one of the highest-volume brands in the world. Fashion at absurdly low prices. The business model had been imitated by many, but never as successfully as the company Mike helped grow to billion-dollar proportions, to the envy of investors who had paid no attention to that market before. Mike had ridden in on the crest of the wave and sold the company three years later for a fortune.

"What have we got today?" Mike asked them with a smile, as they helped themselves to coffee and sat down. As always, they had a variety of new investments to suggest to him, for Mike to consider before they did further research on them. They all agreed in private that they loved working for him. He was a good guy, he expected excellence from them, but he was kind and easy to work for, as long as they produced.

"I had a crazy thought," Renee started. "I went shopping last weekend, at Brooke's. I forget about it at times, because of the location, and when I go down there, it knocks my socks off every time. It's amazing, a treasure trove of high-end brands, and one-of-a-kind merchandise, which is so rare today with globalization. It's family-owned, in a lousy neighborhood. But if you ever want a small jewel of an investment, if you got it out of that neighborhood, moved it to a big new location uptown, and helped it grow into something bigger, you could wind up with something like Chanel or Hermès, even open stores in other cities. It's a goldmine waiting to be discovered. Right now, it's kind of a secret for the elite. Multiply that, and it could be a huge moneymaker." Her eyes were bright as she said it.

"Chanel and Hermès are family-owned too," Joe Weiss reminded her.

"I'd like to be part of those families," Renee commented, and they all laughed, as Mike listened. All three members of his prime research team were in their thirties and full of bright ideas. All of them had gone to top colleges and had had high-level jobs before they came to him, with excellent references and credentials. Renee had gone to Yale undergrad and Harvard Business School.

"It sounds a little precious to me," Mike commented, unenthused so far. "I've heard of it, but I've never been there. Where is it?"

"Sort of south and west of Chelsea. It's been there forever. Two or three generations."

"What's it doing there?" He looked puzzled more than intrigued.

"No idea," she answered. "The building is beautiful inside, looks like nothing outside, and the street is awful, and full of homeless camps now. Inside it's very elegant and distinguished. Kind of old-school, with up-to-date merchandise. It's sort of a hidden secret. People come from all over, but they don't talk about it. I think people who are addicted to it want to keep it a secret. I go there a few times a year. I spend a fortune every time, and love everything I get. The comparison to Chanel and Hermès is a good one."

"Is it profitable?" Mike asked, slightly more interested. That was always the bottom line for him.

"It must be. Most of the merchandise is very high-end, luxury brands. There's a section of less expensive, very chic merchandise, but most of what they sell are very high-flying brands, a lot of them from Europe. You should take a look sometime," she said to Mike. "If you can afford it," she added, and they all laughed.

"It wouldn't be a high-volume investment, like a shopping mall or our low-cost, high-volume brand, but it might be an interesting acquisition, and it might intrigue some of our investors. I have no idea if the owners are looking for investors or want to sell. They may not be interested and be doing just fine without us, but I thought of it when I was there, and I loved the idea. You'd have to get them to expand and move uptown if they'd be willing. Their location now is awful, although it seems to be working for them."

"If they're not in trouble, family businesses are a beast to buy into. They're usually pretty rigid about how they run things if it's working for them. They may not want to grow and move uptown," Mike said.

"And make more money?" Renee looked startled. "Who wouldn't want to do that?" she commented, as Mike jotted down the name of the store. He wanted to ask his mother and daughter about it. Jennifer loved to shop and knew every store in New York, and his mother knew the fashion business from the inside, although she didn't carry high-end luxury brands at her online store. The low prices had been the secret of her success.

"You'd be surprised. Family businesses aren't always about money," Mike answered her, and they moved on to three suggestions offered by Joe Weiss. They were mineral deals in the Pacific Northwest, and an interesting oil deal in Norway. Will only had one biotech suggestion. It was a short meeting, and they left Mike's office an hour later to start their day. Mike had given Joe the green light to research the oil deal, and one of the mineral opportunities, and had discouraged Will from pursuing the biotech deal. They had others that were more lucrative at the moment. Renee had half a dozen other options she was working on, but they weren't far enough along to present to him yet. They were a busy group of bright young minds, always on the hunt for new investments for him and the people who invested with him.

Mike had lunch with one of their major investors, a land developer in Oklahoma who had made a fortune in oil, thanks to Mike. He had meetings after that for a company they had bought and which was about to go public after four years of grooming, and at the end of the day, before he left the office, he called his mother. She was still at her office at seven o'clock and was pleased to hear from him. He didn't call her often but tried to have dinner with his parents every few weeks. Neither of his parents had slowed down despite their ages. And he had the same constitution they did. Mike had been full of energy since he was a boy, and his sister Stephanie claimed they all wore her out. Older than Mike, she worked for their mother, had two sons in college, was divorced, and had a boyfriend Mike liked who owned a construction firm. The whole family admired industrious people and were hard workers.

"Hi, Mom," he said easily. "You're working late." He got on well with his parents and had always hoped to have the same kind of relationship with his own children. He enjoyed spending time with his kids, but he was always being painted as the bad-guy absentee father at home, which didn't help. And he missed them now that they were gone.

"We've got a million orders to fill, and our computers were down for three hours today. I'll be here all night," Beverly explained.

"You work too hard." But he had a feeling it

kept her young. "I have a crazy question to ask you. Have you ever heard of a store called Brooke's? It's somewhere downtown in a dicey neighborhood."

"Oh my God. I haven't been there in years. My grandmother took me there when I was a young girl. She bought a beautiful hat. They had a full custom millinery department. That was years ago. I haven't thought of it in ages, and I haven't been there since. Years ago, I couldn't afford it, and now I just shop online. It's easier, at least that's what I tell our customers. Are you buying it? It used to be owned by a very elegant older man. He stopped to say hello to my grandmother, and he was very charming. I still remember him. He must be dead by now. They must have sold the store."

"Apparently not. The researcher who mentioned it to me says it's family-owned. Apparently, it's still in the same place. His son must be running it."

"It's a very special store," his mother said, remembering it. "I can't believe it's still there. I had forgotten all about it. What would you do with it?"

"Probably nothing. It sounds too small-scale and specialized for us. Something one-of-a-kind like that is too limited. Low-cost, high-volume is a better opportunity," which Beverly knew too, as she had been an econ major in college. "Renee in my office thinks we should invest in it, move it uptown, make it bigger, and open branches across the U.S. Too big a project for too little return," he said simply. "But I was curious about it. She said the same thing as you, that it's a very special place."

"It was." Beverly Weston sounded nostalgic, and Mike smiled.

"I'll have to stop by sometime. Don't work too hard, Mom. I'll call you for dinner with you and Dad next week." Maureen had never warmed to his parents, which had always bothered him. Hers were much fancier, and her father had built a new fortune on old money. Mike's parents had started from nothing and were simpler people. Maureen's father had respected that. She and her mother never did.

"We're going to Palm Beach for the week. Your father says we need a vacation. Maybe he does, but I don't see how I'm going to get away," Beverly told her son, sounding distracted.

"It'll do you good too. You both work hard." He hung up a few minutes later. He always admired his mother and the huge success she had made of her small company. It was mammoth now, and she still kept an eye on everything. He came by his work ethic honestly. Both his parents worked diligently. He was glad they were going on vacation. He wouldn't have minded a week in Palm Beach himself, but he didn't have time. He had meetings booked solidly for the next three weeks, and more to do after that. There were always exciting new developments in his business.

Maureen was out when he got home that night. She didn't leave a note. She never did. If she was out, she was out. It didn't matter where. They rarely ate dinner together, except on an impromptu occasion when they met in the kitchen, foraging for something to eat. She didn't like making dinner plans with him, because she said he was always late, or canceled at the last minute if something came up, which happened more often than not, some conference call from another time zone that he wanted to take at the office.

Mike found some cold chicken in the fridge and made a salad to go with it. He ate at the kitchen table, and answered some emails and texts afterwards, and then looked at his watch. It was still early in California, and he decided to call Jenny, his daughter. He hadn't spoken to her in three days. She loved her college life at Stanford, the classes she was taking, and the friends she had made there.

Jenny answered as soon as she saw Mike's name come up.

"Hi, Dad. I was just thinking about you. I was going to call you later. I figured you might still be at work." It was nine o'clock in New York, which said a lot about his habits.

"I'm home. How's life in the Wild West?" She smiled. She loved talking to her father. He had been busy a lot of the time when she was growing up, but she admired his work ethic and his success, despite what her mother said about him, that he didn't care about anyone but himself, and that his family meant nothing to him. She hated it when her mother said things like that about him. It had put a wedge in her relationship with her mother, much more than with her father. She was his staunchest defender, which made her mother even angrier at Jennifer and her father. She wanted the kids to be as angry as she was and support her position.

"It's not so wild," she answered him. "I've been in the library all week."

"Trying to meet guys, or studying?" he teased her. She was a diligent student and had graduated from high school at the top of her class with honors. She took after him, and he knew she'd be a fine lawyer one day. He might even hire her to work for him.

"Very funny, Dad. Studying, obviously." She'd had a boyfriend the year before, but the romance had been brief. She was a pretty girl, and looked like Mike, with shiny dark hair and cornflower blue eyes. His were more of a sapphire blue and his hair was thick and almost jet black, with only a few stray gray hairs peppered through it. He looked younger than he was.

"I'm sorry to hear it," he said, and laughed, then thought of something. "Have you ever heard of a store in the city called Brooke's? It's downtown in a seedy neighborhood, and I guess it's been there for ages. Your grandmother was telling me tonight that her grandmother took her there as a young girl."

"Oh my God, Dad. It's the coolest ever. It looks like nothing from the outside. Inside, they have the best stuff I've ever seen. I went there with Mom once. It's super expensive, but everything is really beautiful. They have special one-of-a-kind stuff and the fancy luxury brands. Are you buying it?" she asked, and he laughed.

"I don't just go around buying stores. Maybe I wanted to shop there."

"They have cool men's things too. If you buy it, I want a big discount. I can't afford it on my allowance."

"We'll go together sometime. Someone mentioned it today at work, and I was curious if you'd heard of it. I don't know how I managed never to hear about it," although he wasn't a big shopper, he never had time.

"It's kind of like a fabulous secret." Jenny endorsed her grandmother's description of it, from a younger generation, which intrigued him. Whatever the Brooke's style, the store seemed to leave a lasting impression on anyone who went there, even once. It made him curious to see it for himself, not even as an investment, but just intrigued by what his mother, daughter, and researcher had said.

Mike and Jenny talked for a while longer about her classes, her roommate, and the summer internship she had landed, although it was only March. He was going to miss her during the summer, but she was coming home for a month before going back to Stanford for her junior year.

"Have you heard from Zack?" he asked, worried about his son, the great adventurer, wandering around Europe.

"I had a text from him a few days ago. He was back in Munich. He said the sausages and the beer gardens are great."

"Sounds like a very cultural tour he's on," Mike said with the usual tone of concern when he spoke of his son.

"He's fine, Dad. It's good for him to figure things out on his own."

"That's what your mother says. I just hope he figures out that going to college is in his plans for next year. He should have applied by now."

"Maybe he applied from Europe," she said to calm her father. She knew he worried about Zack, and she did too. But maybe he'd grow up during the time he was away. Zack was different, and never wanted to do what everyone else did. He had to find his own path. Their father was a tough example to follow. He had been so successful at a young age. Jenny was sure her brother would figure things out eventually. And he was loving Europe.

Mike was smiling when he hung up. He loved talking to his daughter. She was so levelheaded and sensible and mature for her age. He didn't worry about her the way he did about Zack, who was always a little lost and out of step.

Mike was in bed falling asleep when he heard Maureen come in. But he was too tired to get up to say hello to her, and he guessed that she didn't want him to anyway. He would see her in the morning before he left for work if she was up early enough. If she wasn't, they'd catch up sooner or later. As he thought that, Mike fell asleep, alone in the guest room bed, where he was happy to sleep on his own and have the room to himself.

Chapter 3

Mike was in a cab on his way uptown from his apartment on lower Fifth Avenue, just a block from Washington Square. He liked living at the edge of the Village. He always thought it was too bad none of his kids had wanted to go to NYU, since it was only a few blocks away. Maybe Zack would apply there.

He had left the apartment later than usual, after taking a conference call from London. Maureen was still asleep when he left, and he guessed she had read late the night before. She had no reason to get up early, or at any set hour. The cab had gone ten blocks north when he remembered his conversation with Jenny the night before, and with his mother. He Googled the location of Brooke's on his phone and gave the driver the address. They had gone only half a dozen blocks by then. The address was west and a few blocks north of where he was right now, on the southern edge of Chelsea, which was a mix of fashionable renovated houses, and seedy old buildings, some of which had been rebuilt to rent. There were lots of young people in the area, and a few of the old tenements remained. It was a very mixed neighborhood, most of it trendy and fashionable, and some of it not gentrified yet. He noticed a number of homeless people roaming around pushing shopping carts, and a few camped in doorways.

He was surprised by the store when he saw it. It was a rambling old building with turrets that looked like a small fortress. It was weather-beaten, and ugly. From the outside, it looked like an architectural mistake. There were fashionable clothes in the windows, which were well done to catch a passerby's eye. There was a doorman in a neat uniform standing outside the main door, with revolving doors on either side.

He paid the driver and got out of the cab, and the doorman smiled as Mike approached.

"Good morning, sir," he greeted Mike politely. His uniform and cap were impeccable, and he wore a heavy coat with epaulets and gold buttons, which looked military. Just seeing the doorman and the building made Mike feel as though he were going backward in time to a more genteel era of good manners and people who were properly dressed. The female employees he saw as he went into the store were wearing simple black dresses, stockings, and high heels, and had neatly combed hair. It looked like a world he remembered seeing with his mother when he was a little boy. As he glanced around, he saw elegant luxury items beautifully displayed. There was a rich smell of fine leather, and a hint of delicate perfume in the air. It wasn't overpowering, but it was a subtle, fresh, pleasant scent, as he threaded his way among the counters, admiring the goods in the vitrines. It was exactly what his daughter had described, a place filled with extremely handsome things to buy, and as he walked to the back of the store he saw the hat department, filled with pretty hats, and he wondered if that was where his mother had gone with her grandmother to buy the hat she still remembered.

The store was beautifully decorated, with wood paneling, and looked modern. There were handsome chandeliers throughout the main floor. He saw a coat and a jacket he was tempted to try on in the men's department, but he was on a reconnaissance mission, and didn't want to get distracted. He recognized most of the brand names, although some were more obscure European brands, and he could see why Renee loved it and compared it to Chanel and Hermès. There was a pride of ownership that leapt out at him, unlike any comparable commercial store. He could feel the love that the family who owned it had for their store. It was almost like visiting someone's home, and had a warm, welcoming atmosphere.

He went upstairs and saw the neatly laid out departments. Everything he saw looked appealing, and he saw a number of things he wanted to buy.

He was just leaving the men's department, where he had admired a very elegant pair of well-made brown suede shoes. If he hadn't been on his way to work, he would have tried them, but he didn't want to be any later than he already was getting to his office.

He noticed an impeccably neat, beautiful blond woman watching him. She was wearing just a hint of makeup, her hair perfectly combed into a bun, with gold earrings, and high heels with a chic black suit. She was small, and perfectly proportioned, and she approached and asked him if he had found what he was looking for. He assumed that she was a floor manager, since she was wearing the black suit, unlike the uniform dress of the other female employees. The men wore blazers, gray slacks, and shirts and ties. There was no sign of the familiar casual dress of the day, no jeans or sweatshirts or running shoes on the staff. It added to the feeling of another era, and yet everything they were selling was modern, the latest fashion and up-to-date, and the décor of the store was contemporary too, in contrast to the handsome wood paneling, and the vintage architecture of the building. The interior had been modernized very subtly and effectively. The entire atmosphere of the store made it a place where one wanted to linger in the welcoming arms of luxury, which was displayed so well.

"Yes, I did," Mike told the woman politely, as she smiled at him. She had inevitably noticed how handsome he was. She had seen too that he was wearing a well-cut suit that had been made by an expert tailor, and he was wearing well-polished, expensive shoes. She knew quality goods when she saw them. He was exactly the customer she liked to see at Brooke's, one who would appreciate the merchandise they were selling, and the quality of their brands. "It's a beautiful store," he said. "I'm amazed. I've never been here before. Three people told me about it yesterday, and I decided I had to see it for myself."

"We hope you'll come back again now that you've found us. That's how it is with most of our customers. We're a surprise they don't expect, but once they find us, they come back again and again." She had a warm, welcoming smile and big bright blue eyes.

"It's easy to see why." He was admiring how well trained she was, and how warmly received he felt talking to her. She wasn't overly friendly, and she was professional and polite, but she had a kind look in her eyes that struck him too. He could see that she enjoyed her job at Brooke's. "What's it like working here?" he asked her, curious about this magical place, tucked away in Chelsea, and only known to a select clientele. But the store was fairly full, for an early hour of the day. They clearly weren't lacking customers, and he could see several people paying for what they had bought. Business appeared to be good.

"It's wonderful," Spencer answered his question. He had no idea he was speaking to the owner, and she preferred it that way. She expected all her salespeople to be discreet, polite, and professional, and she was the role model for them all. "I love coming to work every day," she said, and he could see that she meant it.

"You're lucky, not many people feel that way about their jobs," Mike said, and she agreed. "I feel that way about my job too," he volunteered.

"Then we're both lucky." She smiled warmly at him, and didn't ask him what his job was.

"It looks like a good-sized staff," he commented, not wanting to leave just yet, and enjoying talking to her. There was something about her that made him want to linger and chat for a few minutes.

"It is. We don't like to keep our customers waiting, so our ratio of sales personnel to customer is higher than most stores. Service is very important to us, and personnel who genuinely enjoy serving people. I can't stand rude salespeople," she said, "which is so common in so many stores."

"I agree. They let you stand there while they talk to their friends on their phones, or aren't helpful when you're looking for something."

"We want our customers to leave satisfied, wanting to come back to us soon."

"Well, I certainly will," he said, smiling at her, having run out of excuses to keep talking to her. He had enjoyed their brief exchange. "I'll come back soon, and my daughter made me promise I'd bring her too."

"We'll be happy to see you both," Spencer said, and meant it. She'd enjoyed talking to him too. He was well-spoken and intelligent. She wondered who he was. He had an air of power and success about him, which he didn't abuse, but it was there, she could easily sense it about him. "Thank you for your visit. Come back soon," she said as he walked away with a last smile at her. He was still thinking about the whole experience as he got into a cab, and was still impressed by it when he got to his midtown office on Park Avenue and saw Renee.

"Well, I can see what you mean," he said, when she stopped to talk to him in the hall. "I had a conference call at home this morning, and I stopped at Brooke's on the way uptown. What an amazing place. Everything about it is perfect. The décor, the atmosphere, the sales staff, the merchandise. It makes you want to stay there all day and buy everything. They have fabulous things. I'd be broke in a week," he said, and Renee laughed.

"I am every time I go there, but I always love everything I get. It's never disappointing when I get it home, and the quality is fantastic. They really pick their merchandise well. And you don't see it on everyone else. A lot of it is one-of-a-kind."

"I spoke to some woman manager, and she said she loves working there. They must be very good to their staff. They are all very pleasant and can't do enough to help you."

"Now you can see why I suggested it yesterday. The place is a gem. I'm not sure how it would fare though if you moved it uptown. Even the building is special and has a kind of magic to it."

"It's been beautifully redone. They must have used a great architect," Mike commented. He had noticed that the finishes were high quality. It was all expensive work.

"They did. The architect was someone from Italy, I think. Or maybe France."

"They don't look like they're hurting for money or customers. The place was busy. What makes you think they'd want to sell, or even need investment money and partners?"

"Wishful thinking, I guess." Renee smiled at him. "I'd love to own it, and you can afford to."

"I can't imagine them selling. The place just reeks of the owners' pride. Why don't you see who owns it now and what you can find out about their financial situation."

"I'll do some digging and see what I can find out," Renee promised, and went back to her office, as Mike went to his. The project sounded like fun to Renee.

Mike had a dozen phone messages and thirty emails when he got to his desk, about various projects the firm was involved in. He forgot about Brooke's for the time being, although when he thought about the brown suede shoes he was sorry he hadn't bought them. But he could easily see why Jenny loved the store, and why his mother remembered it so well fifty years later. It really was a very special place.

When Mike left the store, Spencer walked around for a few more minutes to finish her morning tour and went back to her office. Her CFO, Paul Trask, called her a few minutes later and asked to come to see her.

She greeted him warmly when he walked in, and wondered what he had on his mind. He did an excellent job as their chief financial officer. He was one of her new hires when her father died and she became CEO. He was very effective at running the store's finances, investing her money, and advising her. Paul dealt with Spencer's mother on a regular basis. Eileen continued to get more and more difficult as she got older. She was lonely without Tucker. She was seventy-five now, and not aging well. Physically she was fine, but she was unhappy and depressed and always complaining about something, and terrified the money would run out. She had no faith in Spencer's ability to run the store competently, and was sure she'd run it aground and they'd wind up penniless. That wasn't even a remote possibility, and Paul was patient about reassuring Eileen frequently that all was well.

"How's my mother?" Spencer asked him with a look of concern when he sat down across from her. He had far more patience with Eileen than her own daughter did. But Eileen was much kinder to him than she was to Spencer, to whom she constantly predicted doom, and disapproved of everything she did.

"About the same. The poor thing is so sad. I tried to get her to come into the store for tea, so she could see how well we're doing, and she always refuses. She said it makes her too sad to come here. She says it's not the same without your dad running the store."

"That's true," Spencer said with a sigh. It had taken them five years to get over the bad investments Tucker had made, and recoup most of the money. It was easier to replace the brands he had canceled. And the atmosphere in the store was much warmer and more congenial since Spencer had been running it, and more like her grandfather's time. "She sees disaster heading toward us around every corner. She thinks I don't know what I'm doing." Eileen made no secret of it, and Spencer heard it from her all the time. "She thinks I'm too much like my grandfather," Spencer said with a smile. That was a compliment at least.

"I wanted to come and talk to you," Paul said, "because we're really on an even keel now. The store is doing well, our investments are solid. I'd like to see us expand though, to reach out to new clients, and bring in younger customers. We have the merchandise they want. They just don't know it. I think we should do more advertising. In the press and online. I'd like to see us set up a website people could shop from. Everyone does that now. It's a major moneymaker."

"If we do that, they won't come into the store," Spencer said, worried.

"Some people can't anyway. They live too far away, or they're not well. We'd capture a whole new group of customers with online shopping. Just about every store in the world does that, but we don't. It's fine for the store to look 'vintage' and a little old-fashioned, but we can't afford to be old-fashioned in our marketing practices. I'd really like you to give it some thought. We could even expand into an annex if we can find a building nearby and put certain departments there. But if we start buying real estate, we should bring in an investor." Spencer looked horrified at the suggestion. It had been suggested occasionally over the years that they should consider moving the store uptown, and Spencer was vehemently against it. Her theory was that if she brought in investors, she'd lose control.

"You know how I feel about investors, Paul. I'm not giving up a fraction of a percent of the business. We keep it all."

"An investor, with enough money, could help us expand without straining our own finances." She knew that her P&L statement was looking good, their profits and losses.

"I'm not spending a penny we can't afford ourselves. Bringing in young people is important, and I

84

agree with you. I want to think about online shopping. We'd need more staff to service it. But an annex is an interesting possibility, if we can afford it."

"I like the concept," Paul said to her. "What I don't like is the neighborhood. I'm not sure we can find a decent building here. One day we may need to think about moving uptown if we want to expand."

"That's not even a remote possibility. Brooke's belongs here. It's part of our cachet, and what makes us different. Besides, we own the building free and clear. Why would we give that up, and have to spend a fortune either buying or renting a store uptown? It doesn't make good financial sense."

"Maybe it does. We would carry a lot more merchandise and more lines with a bigger structure to work from. I know these are big issues, Spencer, but they deserve your serious consideration, or we're going to stay too small, and lose a ton of money we could make if you'd be flexible about some of these issues."

"I won't be flexible about moving, or an investor. You can have anything else." She smiled at him. He'd had the same discussion with her before, and always got the same answer. "My grandfather and father didn't have investors," she reminded him, "and the store is much more profitable now than it was in their days."

"That's true," Paul said, "but times have changed, Spencer. We have to expand if we want to keep growing, and we need help to do that. We can't do it alone."

"Then we'll do what we can, without breaking with tradition, or breaking the bank."

"People very commonly give up a percentage these days, even a small one, to bring in an influx of money. That's how it's done."

"Never!" she said emphatically. Paul knew he'd gotten as far as he would for one day. She was adamant about following the model her grandfather had established. Paul thought she did it out of both loyalty and fear, afraid to try something new. She was young, but she was steeped in the past, after growing up at her grandfather's knee, and learning everything from him. They had adored each other.

Paul decided to take one last shot at it on his way out. "From everything I know about your grandfather, he was never afraid of change, and always willing to try innovative techniques. You won't be failing him if you take on an investor. Give it some thought," Paul urged her.

"I have, and I won't," she said, her expression set in stone. He left her office a minute later, hoping that what he had said to her would sink in over time and she'd agree. She was too smart and too good in business not to see things his way eventually. They needed to expand to stay viable in the market, and the only way to do that significantly was with someone else's money. There was no doubt in Paul's mind. Nor in Spencer's.

When Spencer left for the day, she put Paul's disturbing suggestions out of her mind. She was having dinner with Bill Kelly that night. She didn't want to be upset when she saw him.

He usually took her to a neighborhood restaurant, and they went back to her place afterwards. The boys were having a sleepover at a friend's, since it was Friday night, which was one of the rare times she'd let Bill stay late or spend the night. Between her work and her sons, there wasn't a lot of room for him in her life, and he didn't clamor for more than he got. She was careful not to involve him with her children, except very superficially. He saw them occasionally but had never made a big effort to get to know them. Neither he nor Spencer saw the relationship as long-term, and it had already lasted longer than they'd expected. They'd been seeing each other for two years. He was a nice guy but not a deep person. He enjoyed being a bachelor, and was gun-shy about marriage, and so was she after Bart. The relationship with Bill was just something that had happened, and never went too far.

He knew how important the store was to her, although he assumed that she'd get tired of running it one day, and either sell it or find someone else to run it, which showed how little he knew her. He thought of it as more of a hobby for her, not a lifelong passion.

They both kept things light between them, and saw each other about once a week, outside of advertising meetings for the store. He was handsome, and the right age for her, but there was always something missing between them, probably because Spencer knew she didn't love him, and neither did he love her. It was just easy, and nice to get out to dinner once in a while. She worked so hard at the store that she had very little social life or interaction with other adults, except at work. It was nice being out with a man occasionally, even if it wasn't serious. They had always kept their relationship undercover and discreet, because of his connection to the store through the ad agency where he worked. It met their needs for the moment, but there had never been any pretense of a future, and she had recently begun to think they were reaching their expiration date. He had started to bore her. But she had no great desire to replace him either. He was familiar, and she hadn't met another man who interested her since her divorce. Sometimes she thought that Bart had cured her of love forever.

He hadn't been a heartbreak, but he had been a major disappointment. His profound disapproval of her running the store had stayed with her for a long time. She didn't want another man in her life who would try to force her to sell the store. She shuddered at the thought.

Bill came back to the apartment with her after dinner. They had perfunctory sex, which was less satisfying than usual. It had been fun in the beginning, but had become less so and more predictable over time. He didn't spend the night, and she didn't ask him to. She was sorry to notice that she was relieved when he left. She liked the idea of spending the night alone in her bed, and having a quiet morning to herself the next day before she went to work. She always worked on Saturdays, although she went in a little later than during the week. Francine was going to pick up the boys at their friend's house that afternoon. She left for her day off on Saturday evening when Spencer got home, and Spencer had the boys to herself after that and enjoyed that too. She felt like a real mom when she was alone with them, until Francine returned late Sunday night, after spending her time off with her boyfriend. Their arrangement had worked well for seven years.

* * *

On Saturday, after playing tennis, Mike decided to go back to the store to buy the brown suede shoes he'd seen. It was in the back of his mind that he might see the young manager again. He didn't see her, but he bought the shoes, a gray cashmere sweater, and an English tweed jacket he liked, and was pleased with his purchases when he got home. Renee and Jenny were right. What Brooke's carried wasn't cheap, but it was of the finest quality, and he loved what he'd gotten, and would wear it a lot. Nothing they carried was too odd or too trendy or would go out of style.

Maureen had gone away for the weekend, and Mike enjoyed being alone. The chronic tension between them made solitude preferable whenever possible. It was like a brief relief from a dull ache that he had gotten used to, and was surprised when it abated for a short time. He watched a series he enjoyed on TV, and went to bed early. He thought of the young blond manager at Brooke's again, and was mildly disappointed he hadn't seen her, which seemed foolish to him. What would he have done if he had? But she had been such a pretty woman, so well put together, and so pleasant to talk to. She seemed like a happy person, which had made her more attractive. It was tiresome living with

Maureen's bitterness and complaints. But they were married and intended to stay that way, for their children. It seemed like the right thing to do, to both of them. It was one of the few things they agreed on, even though a sacrifice they were willing to make. Maureen seemed to enjoy punishing him.

When he had gone back to the store, he had noticed the neighborhood more clearly. It was frankly ugly, and parts of it even looked dangerous to him. Brooke's really would have benefitted from a better location, and he wondered why they had never moved. The building had charm inside, but as soon as you walked outside, the magic ended. He wondered if they would do better in a more upscale location. It seemed obvious to him that they would.

On Sunday, after he did the **New York Times** crossword puzzle and got most of it, he flipped through a recent edition of **New York** magazine and was startled to see an article about Brooke and Son. There was a photograph of the front of the building with the doorman standing to attention outside, and he read the article and was surprised to learn that the store's current owner was not the founder's son, but his granddaughter, Spencer Brooke. The writer explained that Spencer Brooke had an MBA, was thirty-seven years old, and had been running the store since she had inherited it from her father at thirty. According to the article she had done a bang-up job and had improved their profits considerably since she took over. It said that she had preserved most of the traditions her grandfather had established, while modernizing subtly and effectively, which explained why she had kept the store in the original location. Although the neighborhood was less than desirable, and inconvenient for most of their customers, they kept flocking to the store in spite of it. The article listed some of their most devoted customers and the list was impressive, of socialites, politicians, movie stars. It said that several First Ladies had shopped there and continued to do so.

The article sang Spencer's praises, and when Mike turned the page, he saw a picture of her and stared at it for a minute. It was the beautiful young blond manager he had spoken to, who had been so lavish with her comments about the store and the staff, and he grinned when he saw it. He thought it was bold of her to have been so enthusiastic about Brooke's, without admitting she was the owner. She had been passionate about it, and now he knew why. There was also a photograph of her with her grandfather when she was a child, in front of the store. The article said that she had been groomed to run it by her grandfather, and that her father's tenure had been brief. He had died suddenly, and she inherited the store at thirty. She was quoted about how much the store meant to her, and how much she had learned from her grandfather.

Mike was still smiling when he finished the article. Spencer Brooke was an intriguing woman. Brooke's didn't make sense to him as a large investment, and there was much greater growth potential in the low-cost brands, like the one he'd invested in before, but there was something about the store that had hooked him. It was a fascinating place, with an endearing history, run by a woman who obviously knew what she was doing and did it well. He couldn't decide which fascinated him most, the owner or the store, but now he wanted to know more about both.

Chapter 4

Mike took the copy of **New York** magazine to his meeting on Monday and handed it to Renee.

"The place is bewitching," he admitted to her. "I saw a pair of shoes I liked there when I went the other day. They gnawed at me, so I went back for them on Saturday, and also ended up buying a sweater and a tweed jacket made by an English tailor. I never do that. I spent a fortune and was happy as can be about it when I got the stuff home. The manager I spoke to on the floor the first time turns out to be the owner, who cruises the place every day, checking on things. She sounds like a force of nature. I still think another high-volume brand would be a better investment, but there's something intriguing about this place. See what you can find out about her, and what their profits look like. Maybe it would be fun, as a modest investment, if they're interested in an influx of money to expand."

"I'll check it out," Renee promised. It seemed like an atypical investment to her too, but she loved the idea. There was something so appealing about the store, and she was fascinated by Spencer when she read the article. She sounded like such a strong woman and a decent person. She was only three years older than Renee, but had done so much with the store to honor her grandfather's memory. The article also mentioned that she was divorced and had twin seven-year-old sons. She had a very full plate and seemed to be managing it all. The article also said that her father's regime had been brief and somewhat colorless, and Spencer had put life back into the store when she took over. She was a very attractive woman.

At the end of the meeting, Mike assigned Renee to assess both options, a high-volume, low-priced brand similar to the first one that had done so well for them, and a possible purchase or investment in Brooke's, although he would want the current owner to continue to run it, since she seemed to hold the secret to their success and was apparently part of the magic. Mike was sure that the other option would be a better investment for them, but there was something about Brooke's that had enchanted him, just as it had all their loyal customers, according to the article.

Spencer had her own staff meeting that morning, and Paul brought up the subject of investors again, for all the reasons he had mentioned before. Spencer shut him down very quickly. Their fashion director, Beau Vincent, agreed with Paul, and said so to Spencer. He felt that they needed to develop an online presence and sell through the internet, and he loved Paul's idea of an annex, although finding a suitable building in the neighborhood, not too far from the mother ship, would be challenging. Marcy said she agreed with both of them. Spencer looked annoyed at the end of the meeting, and even more so when her mother called her. Eileen still had a network of secretaries she spoke to who told her the gossip they heard from the various department heads they worked for.

"Why are you looking for investors?" Her mother landed on Spencer's nerves with both feet, as she usually did, with half-truths and rumors.

"I'm not. Paul Trask thinks we should get a big influx of money to make some improvements, and I'm opposed to it."

"Your grandfather and your father didn't have investors," Eileen said in an accusatory tone that was all too familiar to Spencer. She'd heard it all her life.

"Neither will I. Your spies should be more accurate if they're going to give you insider information. I'm not taking investment money. We can manage without it."

"Are you trying to move uptown?"

"No, I'm not," Spencer said, exasperated. Her mother never showed any interest in the store, except to gossip and criticize it, and her daughter. "I wish you'd stop listening to gossip, Mother. The people who tell you that stuff don't know what they're talking about, and it just gets you wound up."

"I'm not wound up. I just want to know what you're up to."

"Why? You never cared about the store while Grampa Thorny was alive, or when Dad ran it. You hated it, and you said so all the time. Why are you always looking over my shoulder, accusing me of something I'm not doing, and criticizing me for it?"

"That's not fair," Eileen complained. "I'm just trying to be supportive."

"No, you're not. You think I'm going to screw up and fall flat on my face, and you want to be the first to know so you can have a front-row seat when it happens. I'm sorry to disappoint you. I'm not taking investors. We're going to keep on doing what we do now and have always done."

"Maybe you should modernize a little," Eileen conceded. "I like shopping online. I'll bet your grandfather would have made that possible, even if your father wouldn't have." Spencer knew she had that right. Her father hated change of any kind. There had been no improvements during his tenure, and too many good things he had eliminated.

She got off the phone as quickly as she could and was exasperated for the rest of the day. She was distressed by Paul Trask's ideas about an investor, and his persistence about pursuing them. They were valid suggestions, but not if it required an investor to make them happen. God knows who they'd get, or how much of a percentage of the business an investor would want. Spencer didn't intend to give up a single percent to anyone. She was certain her grandfather wouldn't have.

Spencer had a dozen problems come across her desk that afternoon, most of them relatively easy to solve, but annoying anyway. And at five o'clock, she got a call from the White House, from the First Lady's personal secretary. She was coming to New York to shop the next day. She wanted to come to Brooke's, but it was a massive project for her to go anywhere on a personal mission, even shopping. Security measures would have to be in place. All employees in the building had to be vetted and cleared by the FBI, or they couldn't be there. The building had to be carefully checked by the Secret Service, and all exits guarded. The First Lady's security detail would prefer if the store would be closed during her visit. And there could be no leak or statement beforehand about the visit to the store, to jeopardize security. The First Lady was landing the next day and wanted to be at the store by four o'clock, so they would have to close early to accommodate her.

After six phone calls between Spencer and the First Lady's secretary, they were able to compromise on a five o'clock visit, so Spencer wouldn't have to close the store too early and upset their regular customers. They would still be annoyed by an early closing, but the First Lady's visit was an honor Spencer didn't want to refuse. She wanted to make it work for everyone, and after the fact, it would be another coup for Spencer and the store to say she had shopped there. Several First Ladies had.

The wheels were set in motion by six that night. Marcy was going to meet with the FBI with all the employee files, Beau was meeting with the Secret Service early the next morning while they checked out the building, and Paul Trask was standing by to help in any way he could.

It was chaos at the store the next day, with confidentiality agreements to be signed by everyone and the Secret Service to satisfy. Spencer assigned four of the best sales staff to help the First Lady choose a dress for an event she was going to, and Spencer herself intended to stand by, to help smooth down all the interactions and solve any problems, without intruding on the First Lady.

Spencer was waiting at the front door when the First Lady arrived. The store had been cleared only minutes before, and all the customers had to leave early, but weren't told why. They were told simply that there was a scheduled private event, which would begin shortly.

In the end, the First Lady's visit went smoothly, with an enormous entourage around her. She found four dresses that she liked and wanted to purchase. To her credit, she insisted on paying for two, and Spencer made her a gift of the two others. She bought shoes to go with them, and a black satin evening bag. She had gotten everything she came for and was delighted. It all went surprisingly well and there were no mishaps. It was a PR victory for Spencer and the store.

She was exhausted when she got home that night, at ten o'clock, and for once she was grateful that the twins were asleep when she got home. She loved spending time with them and putting them to bed, but not tonight. Their personalities were extremely different. Axel was shy and cuddly. Ben was mischievous and more outgoing. They complemented each other and she loved how individual they were. And they loved spending time with her. She still felt guilty when she didn't have enough free time with them on weeks like this.

Brooke's had a security problem of a different kind the next day, when a well-known senator's wife stole a bracelet from the jewelry department and an alligator clutch bag. They were faced with the choice of having her arrested or not pursuing it. Both items were expensive.

Spencer didn't want it all over the press, nor did she want to encourage copycat thefts. Spencer met the senator's wife at the door and had an extremely delicate heart-to-heart conversation with her in a private room they escorted her to. The woman returned the stolen merchandise before she left the store, and Spencer didn't press charges. The senator came himself to escort his wife home, apologized profusely to Spencer, and attempted to press some bills into her hand, which she delicately refused.

She saw Paul Trask, the CFO, standing by looking concerned when they left.

"Don't look so depressed. She gave it all back," Spencer said to him with a smile. The senator's wife had taken a ten-thousand-dollar bracelet after trying it on, but it was already back in the vitrine by then. The senator didn't want to buy it, or the alligator clutch.

"We had a burst pipe in the warehouse an hour ago, while you were dealing with this mess," Paul said. "We lost a hundred thousand dollars' worth of leather goods." He looked seriously distressed.

"Will our insurance cover it?" she asked him softly, as they walked back to her office.

"Yes, with a five-thousand-dollar deductible. It could have been even worse."

"I should have read my horoscope this morning," she said as she sat down at her desk and the receptionist buzzed her to tell her that Francine was on the phone.

"Is everything okay?" she asked when she answered the phone, with a worried expression.

"We're fine," Francine said calmly. "We're at the emergency room at NYU Medical Center. Ben fell off the jungle gym at the park and broke his arm. They just set it, and he has a bright orange cast. He's okay. We're going home in a few minutes."

Spencer could tell from Francine's tone that Ben was next to her, so she sounded upbeat.

"I'll meet you there," Spencer said, as she grabbed her handbag from under her desk. She was anxious to get home to Ben quickly to see him for herself.

"Everything okay?" Paul asked her.

"Ben just broke his arm. I'm going home."

"I'm sorry. I'll walk you out." There was something he wanted to tell her, but he hadn't had time. It was awkward telling her in the elevator, but he had no other choice. Fortunately, they were alone.

"I know you don't want to hear this right now, but I've had some insider information from someone I know in Mike Weston's office, the big venture capitalist and investor. He was in the store recently and he thought it was fantastic."

"And he wants a VIP discount?" She looked stressed. "We don't give them," she reminded him. "All our customers are VIPs." Hermès didn't give them either.

"No, he's interested in talking to us about some investment money. He's exactly what we need, Spencer. Will you please meet with him and just listen to him?"

"No. He'll take half our business and ruin everything. I won't meet with him. I don't want investors." Her voice was sharper than she intended it to be, but she was worried about Ben's broken arm. "I don't want investors. Just tell him no!" She raced across the main floor then, hailed a cab outside, and headed home to the small townhouse in Chelsea that she shared with her boys. Francine texted her while she was in the cab that they were on their way home. Spencer would get there first, but it had been a hell of a day, and she wanted to focus on Ben, and not the store. She put Mike Weston right out of her mind and forgot about him.

Mike was talking to Renee in his office, as Spencer settled Ben into his bed and told him what a brave boy he was. He had already had his twin sign his cast, and he was in better spirits than she was. It had been a trying day, and at times like this, she had no one to lean on. She had texted Bart to tell him about Ben's arm, but she knew he wouldn't come. He never did. She sat and stroked Ben's silky blond hair until he fell asleep. Axel was downstairs with Francine.

"What do you mean she won't see us?" Mike said to Renee with a look of amazement.

"I put some feelers out through a contact I have who knows the CFO at the store. He's all in favor of an initial meeting. He thinks it could be a good thing for the store. She doesn't want investors, and she flatly refused to see us, to even discuss what might be possible. The CFO would like to meet us. But the owner doesn't even want to hear anything we have to say." Renee couldn't say it in terms he'd like any better. Spencer Brooke wasn't interested. No one had ever refused to see Mike Weston, and he looked annoyed for a minute. Then he laughed.

"She must be a very independent woman if she won't even meet us. That's pretty ballsy. I have to hand it to her." Renee was relieved he was taking it so well. That wasn't always the case. This was a new experience for him. Most people begged him to meet with them. No one had ever slammed the door in his face, or refused to open it at all. "Keep trying. Maybe we should just meet with her CFO." But he wanted to talk to Spencer too, and he thought he could convince her. He wasn't trying to take over her business or buy it outright. He wanted to put money into it, have some participation, and leave her in control.

"The CFO won't talk to us without her permission, and she said a flat no."

"Try again," Mike said stubbornly. He wasn't going to give up that easily. All it did was challenge him. Her flat refusal only enticed him more. This was a new experience for him.

Renee left his office to call her contact again, but a meeting didn't sound likely to her.

Ben had just fallen asleep when Bill Kelly called Spencer. He wanted to come by. She felt like she was on a merry-go-round at full speed. Bart hadn't responded to her text about Ben's broken arm, and hadn't called at all to see how he was, and she was upset about that too. He left her to deal with all the hard stuff. Everything rested on her shoulders, the store, the boys, the decisions, the crises, the senator's wife stealing and how to handle it, the loss of a hundred thousand dollars' worth of merchandise damaged at the warehouse. And now Bill wanted to come by.

"I can't," she said, sounding stressed. "The boys are here. It's a school night, and Ben broke his arm today. He might wake up during the night, and it'll be awkward if you're here."

"I can just come over for a while and bring dinner, if you want." She was too tired and stressed to eat, and she hated to say it to him, but it was just too much. She didn't want to talk to anyone, she just wanted to sit on the couch by herself and stare into space. "It sounds like you had a rough day." She laughed ruefully.

"I did. Today was insane. I'm sorry, Bill, I'm too

wiped out to even talk." He was gracious about it but didn't sound pleased. She rarely refused him, but she was too exhausted to move. She ended up falling asleep on the couch without having dinner. Ben woke up twice in the night, and she was glad that she was there alone and hadn't let Bill come over. She finally spent the rest of the night with both twins in her bed until morning.

Ben went to school with his cast, and a marking pen so his friends could sign it. She dropped the twins off at school herself, instead of Francine, and got to the store early.

She had an hour of peace before everyone else would arrive and sat at her desk answering the emails she hadn't read the night before. She was halfway through them when she saw one from a PR agent she knew. He wanted to know if his clients, a famous rock star and his wife, could come to the store. They wanted the store closed for them. She had already done that once that week, for the First Lady, which had been chaotic beyond belief. And inevitably, it had disappointed their customers who showed up and found the store closed. She couldn't do that to them twice in one week. Her regulars were her bread and butter. Although stars were good too. She needed both.

She responded that she would be happy to accommodate them, but it would have to be after hours. They were welcome to come at six o'clock. The agent thanked her and responded that would be fine. It meant that she would have to ask a skeleton crew of salespeople to stay overtime. She emailed Beau Vincent, their fashion director, and asked him to handle it for her.

He walked into her office half an hour later. She had just finished her last email. She thought he was there to complain about the rock star couple, but he had come about something else.

"There's a big charity event at the Met tomorrow night. They're inviting you for free. I know you hate things like that, but I think you should go. They want you at the head table. It's good publicity for the store. You can bring a date." She groaned at the thought.

"I have nothing to wear," she said, and he laughed.

"I think I can find something for you here," he said, and she grinned.

"Do you want to be my date?"

"I'd love to, but I can't. I'm hosting a birthday party for a friend." She didn't really want to ask Bill, after having refused to see him the night before, but she couldn't think of anyone else, and he was good at things like this. He had the right clothes and was usually happy to go to black-tie events. She had taken him with her before, on the rare times she went. "I'll dig around in the designer department, and send a rack up to your office." Beau knew what she liked and what looked good on her. She trusted him to pick the right thing. She didn't have time to do it herself.

As soon as Beau left her office, on his mission to dress her for the Met party, Paul Trask walked through the door. "I'm here to harass you about Mike Weston. He says he just wants to meet you. He loves the store."

"He wants to throw money at us, and get a controlling interest. That's what guys like him do. I don't want to meet him," she said, looking exasperated. "What part of No doesn't he understand?"

"It's a word he's never heard before." Paul smiled at her. "It wouldn't kill you to meet him."

"My grandfather never had investors. I don't want them either. We'll just have to figure out how to implement your expansion program without an investor."

"We don't have the money for it, Spencer. He does. Or a different investor. It would take us years to come up with that kind of money."

"We'd lose control of the store. I can't let that happen."

"We could do so much with an infusion of funds." He looked sad.

"We're doing fine without it," she insisted.

"We're holding the fort. But without it, we can't grow. An investor would safeguard our future."

"Or take it over, or destroy the store, or change it. I'm not going to be the first Brooke to lose the store." Her great-grandfather had lost his in 1929, she wasn't going to be the next nearly a hundred years later.

"I don't see what harm it would do to talk to him," Paul insisted.

"That's what Eve said to Adam about the snake in the Garden of Eden. Let's not talk to snakes."

"He's not a snake. People say he's brilliant and an honorable guy. We could dictate our terms."

"No, Paul, we couldn't," she said gently, but firmly. She was a woman who knew her own mind. And Paul knew her well enough to know he wouldn't change it. He left her office looking dejected. Mike Weston was such a great opportunity to turn down. He was huge.

An hour later, Beau rolled a rack in with five dresses for her to try. She eliminated two immediately. One was bright pink, and he loved it, but he had been almost sure she wouldn't. The second one was black and looked too severe. The other three were more her style. She was immediately drawn to a soft brushed gold gown, which hung simply and draped from one shoulder and molded her figure. It would have to be shortened, but their alterations department could do it in an hour. She tried it on, and it looked as though it had been made for her.

"You look like a goddess," Beau said, smiling at her. "It's perfect." He had brought shoes for her to try with it. And she had a gold evening bag at home that would be a perfect match. There was a soft gold-colored wrap she could wear if she got cold. She had some beautiful pieces in her own wardrobe, which she seldom wore. She had hardly gone to formal parties since her divorce. It was no longer part of her lifestyle. She went to work and spent weekends with her sons. She didn't need an evening gown to have dinner with Bill Kelly. They rarely went anywhere, except to the Italian restaurant near her house. "You look incredible," Beau said, admiring her. "You should get dressed up more often."

"I'd look silly coming to work in a ball gown, and it's a little over the top for the playground with the boys." She smiled at him.

"We have to do something to jazz up your life," he said.

"This is all the jazz I need." But she had to admit the dress was beautiful, and wearing it was going to be fun.

Beau pinned the hem for her and took the dress to alterations, and she called Bill and apologized for the night before. "I need a favor," she said. "Will you go to a black-tie event at the Met with me tomorrow night? I have to go for the store." He only hesitated for an instant, still a little miffed that she hadn't seen him the night before, but it sounded like fun to him too.

"Sure."

"We don't have to stay late." He promised to pick her up, and she went back to her desk. She was all set for the Met. She had a dress and a date. She wasn't going to make a big evening of it. She'd had a long week. All she had to do was put in an appearance for the store, and the dress was a knockout. Maybe it would be a fun evening after all.

Chapter 5

Spencer worked with Marcy and Beau in her office the day of the charity event at the Met. They were confirming their winter buy for the store. The orders had already been placed several months before, but Spencer liked to go over them in detail. Beau had added three new up-and-coming designers from France, and the same high-end luxury brands they always ordered. He was diligent about coming in under the budget, and he had done it again. Marcy, having bought for the store for thirty years before becoming president, always joined Spencer and Beau for their meetings to offer advice and an overview of the coming season. The three of them worked well together. Spencer had learned a great deal from Marcy, and Beau had been a big success as their fashion director since Spencer had hired him away from Neiman Marcus seven years before. Their future winter buy looked exciting to all three of them.

Marcy had just turned sixty-two, but she was as chic and youthful as ever, with her short snow-white hair. She was full of energy and represented them well as president of the store. She was always cooperative and willing to take direction from Spencer as CEO, despite the fact that she had known her as a little girl. At thirty-seven, Spencer was no longer a child and ran the store with a gentle but firm hand, with her eye on the future, and made responsible decisions which had served them well. Brooke's under Spencer's guidance was even more profitable than it had been when her grandfather ran it. She had learned her lessons well in business school.

She mentioned some of the ideas that she and Paul Trask had discussed recently, including long-term expansion and an annex nearby, and Marcy looked concerned.

"Do you ever think about moving out of the neighborhood?" she asked Spencer, and Beau nodded. He had thought of it too. He knew how attached Spencer was to the building they were in because of her grandfather, but there were increasing numbers of homeless people sleeping in front of the building at night, and they got police reports of muggings, petty thefts, and more recently the rape of a woman who lived nearby. "I think it's getting worse," Marcy added.

"So do I," Beau agreed. "It's a lot worse than it was when I started working here seven years ago. The homeless camped outside seem more aggressive when we leave at night." There were a lot of younger ones in the mix, who were clearly on drugs and desperate for money. They didn't bother anyone in the daytime, and disappeared then, but they were back en masse at night, camping outside. None of the employees had gotten hurt, but local residents had, late at night and on weekends. Brooke's security team was vigilant in the daytime, and looked out for the neighbors too.

"It might be good for business if we move uptown," Marcy suggested cautiously. She knew how attached Spencer was to anything her grandfather had set up, and the building was part of that mystique, even if inconveniently located for much of their staff and many of their customers.

"I'd really hate to move," Spencer said. "This building is iconic." Marcy didn't want to argue the point with her, although she thought the problem of their location was bad for business.

"Our customers might like it if we moved farther uptown, maybe even to another historic building with some character. It could bring us a flood of new customers who don't know the store and don't come downtown. Or a location even farther downtown, like to Soho," which was so trendy and fashionable now.

"It would probably cost us a fortune," Spencer said. But it was more about nostalgia for her than money, as they all knew.

After the meeting, Beau gave her a printout about the event at the Met that evening. It was to benefit an art introduction class for inner city kids in the metropolitan area. There were to be three hundred of the Met's most elite and generous supporters at the party. Seats were ten thousand dollars per person, and they had given her two free tickets.

"I wonder why they invited me," Spencer mused as she glanced at it. The guest list of those who had accepted was included on a separate sheet. She didn't bother to look at it, sure that she wouldn't know anyone there. The guests were among the city and the museum's biggest donors.

"You're an important person," Beau said to her. "Brooke's is an institution and a legend. The name has been important in retail for more than a century. I'm surprised you don't get invited to things like this more often."

"I throw everything out," she said sheepishly.

"I'm not going to spend twenty thousand for an evening, even for a charity event. I'd be broke if I did, although it's a good cause."

"Well, have fun tonight. There will be press there and you're going to look fabulous. Who's doing your hair and makeup?" Spencer laughed at the question.

"Same person who does it every day. Me."

"You don't want to get someone to do it? I can set it up for you," he offered.

"I'll be fine." She smiled at him. Spencer had never been someone who loved attention. She preferred to be behind the scenes, in the shadows, not in the spotlight.

She left the store at five to have a little time at home with the boys before getting ready at six, and Bill was picking her up at seven-thirty in a cab to ride uptown. The invitation was for eight o'clock for cocktails, with seated dinner at nine. She hoped they would seat Bill next to her, since she wouldn't know anyone else there.

She was ready promptly when Bill picked her up. He looked dashing in his dinner jacket, black satin bow tie, and impeccable white tuxedo shirt. He cleaned up well and she smiled when he came to the door. Francine let him in. The boys were already upstairs in their room in pajamas, and Spencer was wearing the beautiful pale gold dress.

"Wow! You look great," Bill said, admiring her. She had worn her hair in a loose low bun at the nape of her neck, and the diamond earrings she had inherited from her grandmother and rarely got a chance to wear. They were simple round studs. She had done her makeup carefully and used very little. Her own natural beauty shone through and lit up her face. She was wearing the gold stole over the dress, and the high heels Beau had picked for her. She looked very glamorous, and very different from how Bill usually saw her, in jeans and a sweater after work, or one of the sober black suits she'd worn at the store if she hadn't changed. "We should do this more often." Not for twenty thousand dollars a pop, she thought but didn't say. "I think the owner of the agency is going to be there tonight. He's a big donor to the Met." Bill wondered if Spencer was too. She hadn't told him that the tickets had been given to her for free.

They chatted on the ride uptown. He was always easy company even if they weren't in love. Over the past two years their relationship had evolved slowly, more toward friendship than romance. They both knew they had no future together although they didn't talk about it. She had talked to Marcy about him, and she reminded Spencer that continuing to date Bill was keeping her from meeting someone she might really care about. She was wasting years if she really didn't love him. Spencer knew that they'd have to stop seeing each other one of these days, but she wasn't quite ready to let go yet, and she wasn't on the hunt for a serious relationship. Her life seemed full enough as it was, and love seemed like such a high-risk endeavor. In a way, dating Bill kept her from taking any risks, which suited her.

When they got to the Met, they walked up the long flight of stone steps to the main door, where security guards and young men in tuxedos were checking people in from a list. They had Spencer's name and Bill's, checked them off, and wished them a good evening. There was a crowd of people just inside the main door, waiting to go up another flight of stairs. It took a few minutes to filter through the crowd, to the French Impressionist wing where the party was being held. Spencer noticed the beautiful gowns the women were wearing and was happy she had picked the gold dress. It felt appropriate in the crowd.

Many of the guests were older, as big donors often were. She saw a number of familiar faces she knew from the press, including the mayor and a senator, and several socialites, some of whom she knew were customers at Brooke's. There was no one she knew well enough to go up and speak to. Bill went to get them each a glass of champagne at the bar. There were round tables set up, laden with silver and crystal and fine china, seating charts in various locations so you could find your seat, and there was a dance floor and a band set up. There would be dancing after dinner, which Spencer hadn't expected. She thought the invitation was only for dinner. She hadn't been to a party with dancing in several years. It always reminded her of how much she had loved dancing with her grandfather when she was a little girl.

Bill returned with their champagne and handed her glass to her, as Spencer continued to look around. Bill told her about the famous actress he'd seen at the bar. As she listened, she noticed a tall handsome man with a neatly cut mane of dark hair. He was looking at her, and he smiled. He looked vaguely familiar, but she couldn't think of who he was. A moment later he disappeared into the crowd. The woman at his side was holding a martini and vanished with him.

They milled around with the other guests for an hour and moved toward the tables just before nine o'clock. Everything was on schedule and running smoothly. She and Bill consulted one of the signs on an easel and saw where their table was located. They had been given escort cards at the door when they checked in, and she'd been reassured to see that they were at the same table, but she saw on the chart that they weren't seated together and were on opposite sides of a table for twelve. She didn't bother to read the other names, since she didn't know them anyway.

When she and Bill got to their table, she was surprised to see that the tall dark-haired man was seated next to her. The men were all standing, waiting for the women to be seated. Spencer noticed that the dark-haired man's companion was seated next to Bill on the opposite side. Husbands and wives and couples who had come together were seated at the same tables, but not side by side. The man smiling down at her still looked familiar. She knew she had seen him somewhere but couldn't remember where. She had a feeling it might have been at the store.

Spencer was seated at the head table, to the right of the dark-haired man. He was impeccably dressed in a tailor-made tuxedo she guessed had been made for him in London. She could recognize a custom-made suit anywhere. He introduced himself as Mike, they shook hands, and she sat down and glanced at the place card in front of him, as all the men took their seats, since the last of the women had taken theirs. Her eyes opened wide when she saw the name "Mr. Weston" on his place card, and she stared at him in disbelief, just as she remembered where she'd seen him. It had been at the store. He was Mike Weston, the potential investor she had refused to meet. For an instant, she thought about walking out before the dinner started, but she didn't dare, it would have been too rude. She wondered if he had tricked her into coming, so he could convince her to let him invest in her business. If he had, she would have thought him a total boor to take advantage of a social situation to corner her. She was trapped, seated next to him at the table for the next several hours.

"Did you invite me tonight?" she asked him with a look of shocked disbelief, and he nodded.

"I did," he confessed. "I just wanted to meet you, so you know I'm not a total savage. I actually met you once at the store, but I didn't know who you were. I'm the Honorary Chair, this is a project I care a great deal about. And I give you my word of honor, I will not speak a word about business tonight. This is purely social. I thought you might enjoy it. If we never meet again, if that's what you decide, I promise never to bother you again. I give you my word." She was still staring at him, and she smiled at what he said. He was certainly determined and had given her free seats to a very expensive, glamorous event. She remembered him perfectly now.

"I'm going to hold you to it," she said, "and if you break your promise, I'll leave. But thank you for the very generous seats." It had been an impressive gesture, and he was much more gentlemanly than she would have expected of Mike Weston, although she had heard that he was brilliant and charming, as well as clever in business. "You found a pair of brown suede shoes you liked but you didn't buy them," she said, remembering him distinctly. He had struck her as handsome then, and he had asked her if she liked working there.

"I went back and bought them the next day," he said with a grin, surprised that she remembered. "I looked for you, but I didn't see you. I thought you were some kind of floor manager or customer service person. I asked if you liked working there. You didn't tell me you owned the store, and I didn't know that was you until I saw you in a magazine. I remembered you too. Do you always walk around the store, talking to customers? And that's not business, by the way, it's curiosity, so I haven't broken my word," he reminded her, and she smiled. She was still stunned that he had invited her to the party so he could meet her, since she had refused to see him. It was a bold gesture, and very resourceful, and it worked. They were seated together, and she would be obliged to speak to him for the rest of the evening.

"I walk the whole store once a day, every morning, just as my grandfather did. He taught me to do that. It keeps me in touch with the customers and the staff on their toes. Keeping our customers happy is very important to me. And I'm always available if there's a problem." She lowered her voice then. "The First Lady shopped with us this week. We closed the store for her. She was very nice." She sounded a little awestruck and he smiled. There was a sincerity and an innocence to her which touched him, and she looked even younger than he remembered, and exquisite in the gold dress. And he had expected her to be tougher since she had been so rigid and adamant about not meeting him, even to talk.

"That's quite an honor," he said admiringly, "and smart of you to close the store for her. The security issue must have been a nightmare." She nodded agreement and didn't comment, and she didn't tell him about the senator's wife who had stolen the bracelet and the clutch bag the next day. But she did mention the pair of famous rappers the staff had stayed after hours for the next day. He was amused by that.

"You must meet a lot of interesting people," he said, watching her. She was so beautiful it was distracting, and he had to concentrate on what she was saying. Spencer was wondering if the woman in the severe black dress with the serious expression sitting next to Bill was Mike's date or his wife, but she didn't ask.

Maureen didn't look happy to be there, but she and Mike always went to big social events together. It was the only social life they still shared. They agreed that it seemed more respectable than going alone and kept up appearances with the social set.

Mike finally couldn't resist asking Spencer the question he was wondering about. "Is that your husband?" He nodded discreetly toward Bill, and she shook her head.

"No, a friend. I wasn't sure who to bring, and the fashion director at the store was busy." Mike nodded, satisfied with the response. Apparently, Bill was neither a boyfriend nor a partner, or he thought she would have said so. "I'm divorced, and I have twin seven-year-old sons," she volunteered. "Do you have children?" she asked him, since his business interest in her was a taboo subject. They could ask questions in a social setting that they could never have asked at a business meeting, and he was achieving just what he had wanted, getting to know her as a person since she had been determined to not even meet him.

"I have a daughter and a son. My daughter is a sophomore at Stanford, heading for law school. And when last heard from, my son was in a beer garden in Munich, eating sausages. He's enjoying a gap year in Europe, possibly a little too much." She laughed at his description. "I never thought of taking a gap year. It's very much of this generation. My father would have killed me if I'd taken a year off. And I was too driven at that age to want to, or even now."

"Me too. I was very serious about my studies, and I couldn't wait to get to the store and get to work as soon as I finished business school." He was impressed to learn that about her and remembered reading it in the article.

"I've been reading about your grandfather. He must have been a remarkable man," he said respectfully.

"He was incredible." Her eyes lit up as she said it. "He taught me everything I know about the retail business and our store."

"It's a wonderful place," Mike complimented her, as the servers set down the first course of lobster salad. There was an alternate choice for those who couldn't eat lobster, but they both did. The band had started playing by the time they finished the first course, and he invited her to dance, which surprised her too. If anyone had told her she would be spending the evening dancing with Mike Weston, she wouldn't have believed it, and would have stayed home. But he was lovely to talk to, and she was enjoying getting to know him. She followed him onto the dance floor. He put a gentlemanly arm around her, and they danced through two dances, chatting all the while, and then went back to the table for the main course of filet mignon. It was an exquisite dinner. People expected it for the price.

Spencer and Mike chatted all the way through dinner. They talked about the extensive traveling he did for business. He had been all over the world, and he spoke admiringly of his parents, still working hard. He told Spencer about his mother's internet fashion business, which she loved and had so much fun with, and had turned into such a huge success.

"We need to add shopping online at Brooke's. We haven't done it yet," she said, and he nodded, careful not to break his promise. He didn't want to do anything to jeopardize the evening. He was enjoying her company. He had paid very little attention to the much older woman on his left, who fortunately had been engaged in deep conversation with the man on her left, so he was off the hook, and could enjoy talking to Spencer. He asked her about her sons and if it was fun having twins.

"It is now." She smiled at him. "It was a little hard at first, and I went back to work pretty quickly. They're identical and play tricks on me sometimes, but I can tell them apart. Their father never could, and still can't." He didn't see enough of them to learn the differences, but she didn't say that to Mike.

"You've got your hands full with the store and twin seven-year-olds," he commented, and she nodded.

"I like being busy, and I think you can have both, a challenging job and a family. I've always believed that. And it seems to be working." Her face lit up when she talked about the twins, and it touched him.

"I didn't learn that lesson in time," he said seriously. "I put all my energy into my career, and one day you wake up, and the kids are gone. It takes a toll," he said softly. Spencer had noticed that he and the woman he had come with hadn't exchanged a look all night. There seemed to be no warmth or communication between them, and she wondered if he meant that focusing on his career had taken a toll on his relationship with his children or his marriage, or both, but she didn't want to ask. She noticed that Bill had had a hard time drawing the woman in black into conversation, and had finally turned to the woman on his other side and was talking to her. She was an attractive blonde, and he looked like he was having a nice time. Mike's companion, who Spencer assumed was his wife, stared at Spencer occasionally, as though trying to guess what she and Mike were talking about. Mike danced with Spencer several more times, and then finally asked his wife to dance and she declined. She looked as though she was eager to go home, but the meal wasn't over yet.

The servers had just set an elaborate chocolate dessert down in front of the guests, topped with gold flecks and meringues, when Spencer's cell phone rang in her purse. She always left it on because of the boys, in case there was an emergency at home. She apologized to Mike, took out her phone, and answered, looking worried, as he watched her. She asked a serious of quick, staccato questions.

"When? How did it start? When did they get there? How bad is it?" It was Marcy. She was on the emergency list at the store, as were Paul Trask and Spencer. This time, they had called Marcy first. "I'll be there as soon as I can. I'm still at the Met. Thanks, Marcy," she said, and hung up and looked at Mike with huge, worried eyes.

"Are your boys okay?" He looked worried for her. He could see that she was trying not to panic, as she set her napkin down on the table.

She answered in a low voice, so no one else would hear her. "There's a fire at the store. I've got to go." He could see terror in her eyes and wanted to reassure her.

"Of course," he said, standing up as she went to whisper a few words to Bill to explain. He was having a great time with the blonde next to him, they were both laughing and drinking more champagne, which was being served with dessert. She told Bill about the fire.

"I've got to go. You can stay if you want," she said. "I'll be fine. There's nothing you can do. The fire department is there."

"Is it bad?" He looked concerned, but not panicked.

"I don't know. I hope not."

"You don't mind if I stay?"

"No, don't worry." She patted his shoulder, nodded at the blonde, and hurried back to her side of the table to say goodbye to Mike. She was in a rush. "Thank you so much for a wonderful evening, and for keeping your promise."

"Come on," he said swiftly, "I'll walk you out. Do you have a driver here?" She shook her head as she half ran beside him in the high heels.

"Take mine," he said quickly.

"No, really. I'll take a cab."

"Are you sure?" She nodded, and he hailed one for her and helped her into it, in the long gown and high heels. "I had a great evening talking to you," he said. "Now go. I hope everything will be okay." But it was a very old building, with lots of wood and full of flammable garments. He was worried for her and the store as the cab pulled away, and he walked back inside, thinking about her. She was nothing like he'd expected. He had imagined a dragon from her stern refusals, and she had turned out to be a lamb, in wolf's clothing perhaps, but she was clearly a good person, dedicated to her children, her business, and her grandfather's legacy. He understood much better now why she was afraid of investors who might try to take the store from her. She was the keeper of the flame, the guardian of the holy grail her grandfather had left her. They hadn't talked business all night, but he understood her now, and he liked her immensely. He admired her, which made him even more interested in her store. She was an intriguing woman, of many facets, and great competence he could guess.

The party lasted for another hour, with speeches and thanks and an explanation of the plans for the new program, and then they all got up and the party ended. Mike noticed that Bill left with the blonde, and he had a feeling that Spencer wouldn't have cared, or at least he hoped not. He had already made a quick assessment that Bill wasn't worthy of her. She was an amazing woman, and he didn't deserve her. He seemed like an ordinary guy with nothing special about him.

Maureen made a dry comment in the car on the

way home. "You seemed to be having a good time with the girl in the gold dress."

"It was business. We've been researching investing in her company." He didn't explain that she owned Brooke's. He didn't feel he needed to. Maureen was never interested in his business. "She doesn't want us to invest, she's afraid she'll lose control."

"Smart girl," Maureen said, and lost interest in the subject, as he wondered how bad the fire was, and hoped it was only a minor scare. They went to their respective rooms when they got home, having said good night in the hall.

"Thanks for going with me," Mike said, and she just looked at him and nodded and closed the door a minute later to what was now her bedroom, and no longer theirs.

Chapter 6

Spencer gave the cab driver an extra twenty dollars for getting her home as fast as he could. She paid him and raced inside to change out of her evening clothes. Francine and the boys were asleep as she pulled on jeans, a warm sweater, and running shoes, and raced out again, hailed another cab, and was at the store minutes later. There was gray smoke coming from the roof, which Beau explained meant the fire was in the process of being put out. The fire had been on the top floor that held the restaurant, some of the offices, and the lower-priced department. But there were also locked storerooms where the staff kept some high-priced goods. As well as fire damage, Spencer was worried about water and smoke damage, which could be just as bad.

Marcy and Beau had come, and they stood on the sidewalk with Spencer, talking to the fire chief. He said that the fire had started in the kitchen, possibly an electrical fire, or someone had left something on when they closed the store for the night, and it had burned slowly for hours and then burst into flames. The firefighters weren't sure of the cause yet. The store had lost merchandise. The question was how much. It was too soon to know. The three of them, Spencer and Marcy and Beau, huddled together, waiting for news, and wanted to go inside to assess the damage, but the firefighters said it was still too dangerous to go in, and the fire could become more active again. The risk was not entirely over.

The homeless people who clustered around the store at night had been scattered by the police and had taken refuge elsewhere. It was a grim scene as the charred furniture from the restaurant was thrown onto the street, and the firefighters were still inside hosing things down and causing more damage, although for a good cause. They had to be sure the fire was out and wouldn't reignite. Spencer looked grim as a cab stopped near where they were standing, and a tall man in jeans and a baseball jacket with disheveled black hair got out. Spencer saw immediately that it was Mike Weston. He headed toward her with a serious expression. The other two didn't know who he was, but he was a striking-looking man, and it was obvious that Spencer knew him. Beau raised an eyebrow questioningly at Marcy, and she gave a small shrug. She didn't recognize him either.

"How's it going?" the man asked Spencer in a warm tone of concern, as though he knew her well. He felt as though he did now, and this was an intensely personal moment of fear and worry for her.

"The fire is almost out. We're waiting to assess the damage, but they won't let us go in yet. It started in the kitchen of the restaurant. It was burning for hours before it burst through the roof. Thank God it did, instead of going down to the lower floors. But the smoke and water damage may be bad. We don't know yet. And what are you doing here, by the way?" She smiled gratefully at him.

"I wanted to be sure you were okay, and I don't have your number."

"Thank you," she said softly, and introduced him to her associates, who looked shocked once they knew who he was. They would have questioned her about it, but they couldn't with him standing there. "Mike invited me to the Met party tonight. I didn't know before I got there," she explained to them.

"Or she wouldn't have come," he added, and Beau and Marcy laughed, since they knew the situation and that Spencer had been refusing to meet him. "Hopefully, the damage won't be too bad," he said, and they all nodded. It was two in the morning by then, and he stayed with them until three, when they finally left. They couldn't go in until morning. It was still too hot and dangerous. Mike had stayed with them, and took Spencer home in a cab.

"Do you want to come in for a cup of coffee?" she asked him when they got there. She looked exhausted, and they both had soot on their faces from ash floating in the air.

"You need to lie down and get some rest," he said gently.

"Thank you for coming. I was terrified till I got there. They already had it under control. But the damage could be pretty bad. I don't know how much merchandise we lost. We had a leak in the warehouse last week, now this." She looked beaten for a moment, and he gave her a hug.

"Sleep. It'll look better in the morning. And your insurance will take care of it," he reminded her, and she nodded. Marcy had already called and left a message. "I'll call you," he said, and then remembered that he didn't have her number. She gave it to him willingly, and he gave her his. He had been so kind and compassionate all night. It was amazing how life worked out at times. Only a day ago she had considered him a potential enemy, and overnight he had become a friend. His showing up at the fire had demonstrated that he was a decent human being and a good person. As he left in a cab to go home, she realized that she hadn't heard from Bill all night. He hadn't called to check on her after the party, to see how things had worked out. And Mike had come there to see what he could do to help. Bill hadn't given any sign of life. It was a big statement about how little he cared about her, and it wasn't lost on her.

She went back to the store that morning after she'd slept for a few hours. There was burnt wood and charred furniture piled up in the street. Marcy had called a cleaning crew to take the debris away. They were already working. There were two fire-fighters on the scene who escorted Spencer and Marcy into the building to survey the damage. The top floor was frightening. The other floors had been untouched by the fire. But there was noticeable smoke damage, and some water had gotten to the lower floors. The store would probably have to be closed while they made repairs. The insurance adjuster was coming on Monday morning to assess the damage.

Beau Vincent and Paul Trask came that after-noon, but there wasn't much they could do on their own. They all went to a nearby coffee shop after they had toured the store and surveyed the damage. It could have been much worse, and Spencer was grateful it wasn't. They had just ordered coffee when Beau looked at Spencer with a quizzical eye.

"Excuse me, Ms. Brooke, would you like to explain how Mike Weston happened to show up here last night, acting like your best friend?" She looked embarrassed for a minute and smiled at them. Paul looked like he was about to keel over when he heard it.

"The Mike Weston you've been refusing to meet?"

"The very same," she admitted. "He invited me to the event at the Met last night. He was the Honorary Chair. He sent me two tickets I didn't know were from him and he had me seated next to him. I told him that if he said a word of business, I'd leave. So he didn't, and he was very nice to talk to. He was sitting next to me when I got the call about the fire, and he showed up on his own."

"Are you willing to talk to him now?" Paul asked her.

"Maybe. I haven't decided yet. I'll concede that he seems to be a nice person, but that doesn't mean I want to be in business with him. I'll think about if I want a meeting with him."

"Well, let me know," Paul said, still stunned by the latest development.

They left after that. There wasn't much they could do. She had a text from Mike that afternoon when she got home, just asking how she was, and offering anything he could do to help her. He had been nothing but kind since they met. He wasn't at all like what she had expected.

She didn't hear from Bill until ten o'clock that night, and she was profoundly shocked by that. He called her while she was lying on her bed, watching TV, trying not to worry about the store. It had been a deeply upsetting twenty-four hours, with no word from him.

"So, how'd it go last night?" he asked blithely, as though inquiring about another party she'd gone to after the Met.

"How'd it go? My store was on fire and we lost most of the top floor and the roof, with water and smoke damage on the other floors. How do you think it went? It didn't occur to you to call a little sooner? Mike Weston showed up to help us, and I only met him last night. We've been dating for two years and you couldn't give me a call?" She was angry at him.

He sounded instantly uncomfortable. "Sorry, Spence, I was busy."

"Doing what? If your house caught on fire, I'd call you."

"I'm calling now, and it wasn't your house. So I

141

knew your kids were fine, it was just the store, and you said I didn't have to come."

"You could have called."

"True. I didn't think of it till now." He was honest although not impressive. "And you and Weston looked cozy last night. I thought you hated him."

"I do. I did," she corrected herself. "He's a nice person. That doesn't mean I want to be in business with him or give up my store."

"His wife is a total beast. She was pissed off all evening. She said she hates going out with him. She hates a lot of things. It was like talking to an angry porcupine all night."

"You seemed to hit it off with the blonde on your other side," she commented.

"Yeah, I did," he said in a noncommittal tone, and Spencer had the feeling that he'd spent the night with her, which was why he hadn't called. She didn't ask, and didn't want to know. His not calling or showing up for the fire told her all she needed to know.

"I think we've about done it, Bill, don't you?" There was a long silence at his end. It was what he wanted too, but he hadn't expected her to be so direct, so soon. He wanted to see the blonde he'd spent the night with again. It had been an incredible night for them.

"I guess you're right," he said cautiously. "I

thought we had a little more mileage left in us," he said. But not Spencer, after the fire. He was just too cavalier and disengaged. What was the point of being with someone who cared so little about her?

"I don't think we do," she said coolly.

"I hope the agency doesn't lose the Brooke's account because of me," he said. It was all he could think of now, and that he'd get fired if they lost the account. But Spencer wasn't a vengeful person, he couldn't see her doing that.

"Don't worry, they won't."

"I guess that's it then," Bill said, and Spencer sat quietly for a minute. It had never been a big love affair and she wasn't even sure she'd miss him. His not showing up for the fire, or even calling, finished it for her.

"Bye, Bill," she said softly and hung up. And thus ended two years of dating Bill Kelly, as quietly as that, without a tear.

Marcy rented a temporary office, where she, Spencer, and Beau met on Monday to discuss the fire situation. The insurance adjuster had assessed the damage, which was considerable, but not nearly as bad as it could have been. The store staff had to do an inventory of the damaged items. The construction company had come by to assess what needed to be rebuilt and promised to give them an estimate by the end of the week. Mike was right. Now it was all about insurance. And they had to replace lost merchandise, if they could. Beau was working on orders based on what they'd seen. It was going to be a costly business, and the store would have to be closed at least part of the time during construction, meaning a loss of revenue, which they had insurance for too.

"And more bad news," Paul said with a grim expression. "We had another leak in the warehouse and lost another fifty thousand dollars' worth of merchandise. Add that to the leak last week for a hundred thousand and the fire damage, and Spencer, I hope you're willing to at least talk to Mike Weston now. We need money, and not just from the insurance people. We want to expand, in order to look to the future, and now we're going to be closed for a month or two and we have to rebuild. Now's the time to really look at our needs, see what kind of money we require, and how best to get it, and from whom. Mike Weston may not be the answer, but someone will have to be," he said somberly, as Spencer listened.

"I'll meet with him once and see what he says. But just because I sat next to him at the Met and he showed up at the fire does **not** mean I'm going to turn the store over to him. Let's be clear on that.

You set it up, and I'll meet him. But I'm not giving up my business to anyone."

"We need to think about moving too," Marcy added. "I know you don't want to," she said to Spencer, "but at some later date, it might be the smart thing to do." Spencer looked miserable when she said it. It was the last thing Spencer wanted to do. And she wanted even less to take on a partner.

Paul said he'd set up a meeting for her with Mike Weston as soon as they got organized after the fire, which wouldn't take too long at the rate they were moving. Since she knew Mike now, and he had been kind to her, she was willing to at least listen to him.

Paul made the appointment for the meeting, at Spencer's request, at the store. She had taken a basement storeroom and turned it into an office, so she could be on-site to see what was going on with the removal of debris, and the reconstruction. The contractor had estimated eight weeks. In the meantime, Spencer wanted to see everything that was happening. The meeting was set for the week after the fire. Mike met with his team about it before he met with her. He wanted all the figures available to them, and everything they could lay hands on, so he could understand Spencer's needs even better than Spencer did, and that way he could make intelligent suggestions, in her best interests and his own. He wanted to offer a short-term plan and a long-term one, and hear her thoughts about them.

He came to the meeting with a briefcase full of research, and Spencer came to it with her intimate knowledge of the store. She had all the current figures in her head.

She looked tense in the grim basement office without a window, when Mike arrived for the meeting, looking friendly and relaxed. This was obviously one of the things he did best. Negotiating was not her strong suit, especially when she felt threatened. But at least she was on home turf. Paul had offered to join them, and she declined. Now that she knew Mike, she wanted to meet him face-to-face, alone. She thought it would go better. She handed him a mug of steaming coffee and they began.

She listened carefully to what Mike envisioned for her, given what he'd read and studied so far. What struck her immediately was how bright he was. He really was brilliant, just as people said of him. And he seemed like a straight shooter, which she was too. They were two smart people meeting on a level playing field.

"First of all, you need a well-set-up online business, with all the merchandise you have in the store, and maybe some special opportunities as an incentive. And you need that right away. It will double your sales overnight.

"Next, you need to find a way to expand. I think the annex Paul Trask suggested is just a patch on a leaky tire. It's a half-assed solution that will be complicated to run, and more of a headache than an asset. I think you need to move to a bigger facility, and move out of this neighborhood, either uptown or down. But you need to get out of here. It's dangerous, for your customers and your employees. The police reports on this area are alarming, particularly on this block, we checked. You need to get out while you can. You can sell the building, not at a huge price, but you'll make some money on it, to put toward a bigger store somewhere else. Those are the two biggest changes that I think need to happen. Then you can fine-tune it later. You should probably look at a new warehouse facility too. The one you have is leaking like a sieve and that's costing you money too.

"You need an influx of money to accomplish those things. You can borrow from a bank, but they won't give you as much as I will. We can both figure out exactly what you need, and I'd be willing to commit what you need to do this right."

"And what would you want in exchange?" she asked him directly in an even tone. She was calm after listening to him. The conversation hadn't been heated so far. It was honest. They were both straightforward people.

He didn't hesitate before he answered. "Normally, with an investment this size—and it will be sizeable, if you include the cost of buying a new building, and not a small one, in an upmarket location—in most cases, in that kind of range, where the money is at your disposal as you need it, I would want full control, or at least majority control. It gives us some leverage to help you run the business and see things our way. But I know how much this business means to you, and why. The deal will never happen if I try to take control. I know how much you don't want that. I would be willing to accept forty percent ownership, which would leave you majority control, because I trust you, for two years, with a set or sliding amount in two years, which would give me majority control then. I'd say an amount somewhere between twenty and forty percent more, depending on how well you're running the business."

"So, what you're saying is that after two years, you would own either sixty or eighty percent of the business, and I would have minority participation."

"Yes, that's what I'm saying, and we would want you to stay on with a contract to run it just as you do now. We could settle on a number you're happy with. And long-term, I think you could open several stores around the country, if you have good people to handle the merchandise, and that would be a big moneymaker for you too."

"But whatever I do, I'd get the money from you now to make all these changes, but two years from now, you'd be the majority owner, and I would only have between twenty and forty percent ownership?"

"That's correct." He looked her straight in the eye as he said it, hiding nothing.

"I can't do that. You know I can't. I'm not going to give up ownership of my store. That's why I didn't want to meet with you in the first place. I agree with you about the online shopping. We have to do that, we're way late with that. I should have done it before. And you may be right that an annex would turn into a problem. But I don't want to move uptown, or downtown. We're not ready to do that, and because of the money it would cost, I would sell myself into slavery to you, and you would own the store. That doesn't sound like a good trade-off to me. And it may be somewhat dangerous down here, but none of our customers or employees have gotten hurt so far. Some of the residents have, but no one in our Brooke's community. Mike, I can't take the deal you're offering me." She looked sad. It was everything she had expected him to say and didn't want. He didn't look surprised.

"Will you think about it?" he asked her gently.

"No," she said. "It's the definition of everything I won't do. And it's not what Brooke's is about. I don't want to be a big uptown department store. And if you have control, who knows what kind of merchandise you'll force us to carry. We're a luxury brand specialty store, with many one-of-a-kind items we travel the world to find, which is why people come here. I'm not going to sacrifice that, not for what you describe, which would be my worst nightmare. We can't make a deal, Mike. There is no offer here of any interest to me."

"You could lose your business one day and go under, because of the changes you're not willing to make now." He was trying to scare her, but it was also a real possibility.

"We've been in business for seventy-three years. I figure we might last a while longer, doing things our way. My grandfather taught me to fight for what I believe in, and that's what I'm doing every day. I'd love to have your money to make some big improvements here. But not at the price I'd have to pay. I might as well sell you the store outright today, instead of waiting two years to have you take control of it then."

"That would be a possibility too," he said. He wasn't trying to insult her. This was business, and he was a smart businessman. He was looking for the best deal to serve his own interests, not hers, and she knew it.

"You would ruin it," she said, standing. "The store isn't for sale, Mike, and I don't want a majority partner. I think we're done here." He stood up and looked at her regretfully. Once he knew her, he had suspected it would come to this. "Thank you for the offer, which I gratefully decline."

"Let me know if you change your mind," he said.

"I won't," she said, and he walked to the door and closed it quietly behind him. There was no deal to be made.

Mike advised his team that afternoon of the outcome of the meeting with Spencer.

"There's no deal possible," he told them simply. "She won't give up control."

"She needs the money," Joe Weiss said, "or it'll strangle itself eventually. If she can't expand, it'll just die on the vine."

"She won't let it. At worst, it'll stay an unusual specialty store, the way it always has been. She doesn't want the kind of expansion we're offering her, or what it would cost her in control. In a way, I admire her. She's a gutsy woman. She has a dream, and she won't give up on it. It's a legacy she's guarding with her life. For us, there's no deal possible. We need to move on. Let's look at that high-volume, low-cost brand we were considering in the Southwest. Brooke's is over for us," he said firmly, but as they moved on to other possible investments, Mike felt strangely sad to let Brooke's go. He wanted to help her, and he had no excuse to see Spencer anymore. He had only seen her four times in his life and he already knew that he had never admired anyone as much. She was an honorable woman to the very depths of her soul. She brought out the best in him, and he was going to miss her.

Spencer was thinking of Mike too after he left the store. There had been no surprises in what he said to her. What he described was exactly what she had feared and had rejected all along. What he had suggested made total sense for him, and none for her, unless she wanted to change Brooke's completely. But it had been an honest offer for someone who wanted to get rid of the burdens and responsibilities of the store, which she didn't. She loved the store to the very core of her being, like a person or a child. She was glad she had met Mike Weston. She recognized that he was a very special man, but there was no way she would ever do business with him, and make a deal. For Spencer, the dream she had was still intact and worth fighting for.

Chapter 7

Mike was testy and on edge for the week after Spencer had turned down his offer. He wasn't surprised, since he recognized that the deal was stacked in his favor, but he was disappointed. He realized now how unrealistic he had been, trying to talk her into it. She was never going to accept his offer, and she had said so all along. She was above all an honest woman. He admired her more than he had expected to, and in particular her passion about what she believed in. She set herself impossible goals and expected to live up to them. He respected her all the more for that. And now he had no reason to speak to her. He was startled to realize he missed her.

He had had arguments with his entire research team that week, which was unlike him. He was usually even-tempered and good-natured, but he wasn't now. He was irritated by the other investments they presented to him. They all seemed lackluster and uninteresting, and nothing to get excited about, even if they were likely to be profitable. Ridiculous as it seemed, even to him, he missed Spencer, a woman he barely knew, who had her own life and problems to deal with.

He often wondered how she was faring with the repairs after the fire, and wished he could have helped her. There was no question that a large influx of money from him would have made everything easier for her, but there was no way he could make a deal, and such a small one by his standards, without having majority control. He hoped that she understood that and that it wasn't personal. He had been completely up front with her, as he always was. She had been as well, refusing to sell her family legacy to a stranger who would then control it, no matter how efficiently. One day it would no longer be her company, or her family's, it would be his. Her grandfather had passed her the baton, and there was no way she would drop it or abandon it. It was to her credit, in his opinion, that she had stuck to her guns, so any deal between them was impossible, no matter how much fun it might have been to work on it with her. An investment of that size, for him, would have been a sidebar. But he did love the store, and admired how she ran it. There was so much he admired about her, and now she was lost from sight. He would have felt like a fool admitting that he missed her. He barely knew her. But she had haunted him since they met. He loved the contrast between the glamorous way she looked at the Met party, and seeing her in jeans with her disheveled hair and her smudged face the night of the fire. She was a real person.

He had his own problems too. He was worried about his son Zack floating around Europe. When was he going to get his act together and go back to school, and find a career path he wanted to pursue? Mike was tired of Maureen blaming him for putting too much pressure on his son. If he didn't, who would? It was time for Zack to come home. He had been gone for eight months, and he seemed no closer to finding a direction than he had when he left. And Mike worried about him being so far away.

He'd been trying to reach Zack for three days, with no response, and complained about it to Maureen when he saw her in the kitchen one night, while they both dug in the fridge for something to eat for another dinner they wouldn't eat together. He was tired of that too. There was a lot he was tired of these days. And Maureen's constantly hostile, critical attitude was high on the list.

They sat down at the kitchen table at the same time, each with a salad. They no longer ate meals together, except if they turned up in the kitchen at the same time. And when they did, they rarely talked. More often than not, she read a book, or her texts, so she didn't have to talk to him.

Their going to the Met party together had been a rare exception. They only did it because they didn't want the people they knew socially to suspect that their marriage had fallen apart. Maureen had agreed to go, grudgingly and with a long face, but she was there.

"Have you heard from Zack?" he asked her when she sat down. "He's not answering me. I don't like it when he does that."

"Then stop bugging him about going back to school," she snapped at him. "Maybe then he'll want to talk to you."

"I asked him if he needed money. That usually works," he said caustically. Mike had come to hate who he had become with Maureen. He had begun speaking to her the way she spoke to him, which was hateful. They brought out the worst in each other and had for years. Hers was because she was so bitter and resentful, and his responses were a reaction to hers. Whatever the reason, it was a miserable way to live, or treat another person, or be treated.

"He was going to Amsterdam after Munich," she said in a more neutral tone.

"I don't like his going there, with the 'coffee shops.' They'll be stoned the whole time they're there. It's the only reason they wanted to go."

"That's not true. There are some wonderful museums there," she said naively.

"You have more faith in our son than I do," Mike said. "That's a lot of temptation for three eighteen-year-olds. When are they going back to Paris, or London?"

"I don't know. Soon," she said. "That's the whole point of his being there. He's not on a schedule, and he doesn't have to answer to us." But Mike thought he did. He was just a kid.

"He needs to come home. Don't you worry about him? I worry about him all the time."

"That's because you don't have faith in our children," she said, accusing him again. Whatever he did or said was always wrong.

"No. It's because I was an eighteen-year-old boy once too. They do dumb stuff. And I was tamer than most."

"So is he," she said calmly. "If you'd just get off his back, he could prove it to you. He's a great kid."

"I know he is, but the world can be a dangerous place, especially today. And he's far from home."

"He's done fine for eight months." That much

was true, but Mike worried anyway. He felt better when the kids were at home. He worried less about Jenny, in the regulated structure of Stanford, living in the dorm. She was more mature and less adventuresome than her brother, although they were only a year apart. "You know, you ruined Zack with all the pressure you put on him to achieve," Maureen said, as Mike finished his salad and felt a fist clench in his stomach. He hated it when she said things like that. He felt instantly guilty, with a terror that she was right.

"I'm trying not to do that anymore," Mike said quietly.

"It'll take him years to recover, if he ever does."

Mike couldn't stand it anymore. Added to the malaise he was feeling over the deal with Spencer Brooke going sour, having Maureen heap guilt on him again over their children was just too much, and more than he could tolerate at the moment. He not only felt that he had failed his children, but he felt now as though he had failed Spencer because he couldn't make the deal work for her.

"Are you talking about Zack or yourself?" he asked Maureen across the table. She hesitated before she answered.

"Maybe both. You were never there for me when it mattered, or the kids."

"I know, you've said it a million times, and I'm

so tired of hearing it. There's nothing I can do about it now. How long are you going to punish me for that?" He was serving a life sentence with her for his crimes. "Is this really how you want to live? In separate rooms, blaming me for everything that's gone wrong in your life? What's the point of that?" He was feeling desperate while he talked to her. It never got better, only worse.

"You were a lousy husband and father, that's not my fault."

"No, it's not," he admitted, "but I can't rewrite history. I can only try to do better now. But you never let that happen. You'd rather beat me up for the past. I didn't beat you, for God's sake, or abandon anyone. I was out making a living, to give you all a good life. And you're going to punish me forever. We don't even talk to each other anymore."

"I have nothing to say to you," she said coldly.

"Then why are we still married? What are we doing here? If we live another forty years, is this what we have to look forward to?"

"What do you expect after twenty years of marriage? Hearts and flowers? That all died years ago because you were never around." Oddly enough, he had been faithful to her, not that she cared.

"I think our marriage died when I wasn't around," he said in a tight voice. He'd had enough. "And maybe I do expect hearts and flowers, or a conversation or a smile when I come home. We live like strangers, Maureen. Or enemies, which is worse. I can't do this anymore. I don't want to. What are you trying to prove? How much you hate me? How bad I was, how indifferent we can be to each other? You're never going to forgive me, are you?" She thought about it and shook her head.

"No, I'm not," she said.

"Maureen, then I'm done," he said in a choked voice, but he was aware of a sense of relief when he thought about it. She was never going to let him out of jail. He could see that now. He had to free himself. He had nothing better to go to, and no plan, but there had to be a better life than this. He had wanted to build what his parents had, and he and Maureen had failed abysmally.

"What are you going to tell the kids?" She didn't argue with him about it or beg him to stay.

"I'm going to say that it's very sad, but our marriage died somewhere along the way, and we love them, but we can't live together anymore. They're old enough to understand, and they've seen it themselves."

"Ending it is your idea," she said accusingly. It was another thing to blame him for.

He nodded. "It is. It'll be healthier this way, for both of us. I don't want to be your whipping boy anymore. We both deserve a better life than this." He felt less sad about it than he thought he would. He felt like he was getting out of prison.

"Do you want a divorce?"

"Maybe. I don't know." It had all just suddenly become too much. "I'll look for an apartment and move as soon as I can." She didn't try to stop him, and he suspected that she was relieved too. Maybe this was what she'd wanted all along. "You can have whatever you want," he said, and stood up and looked at her. "I loved you, Maureen, I really did, even if I wasn't around all the time. I thought I was doing something good for all of you. And you're still my family. I just don't want to be punished for the rest of my life." She nodded and stood up too.

She didn't respond to what he'd said or tell him she loved him. She didn't, and hadn't in a long time. He knew it too. "When should we tell the kids?" was all she asked.

"I don't know. I didn't plan this. It just happened while we were talking. Maybe we should have done this a long time ago." But at least they had stayed together long enough for the kids to grow up and leave home. "I don't think we should tell Zack till he comes home. He might be upset. Do you want to tell Jenny?"

"No, you can." Maureen didn't get along with her daughter either. She was hard on her, and soft on their son, which never seemed right to Mike. Jenny knew it too.

Mike looked at apartment rentals online in the guest room that night, and wrote down some numbers to call. He felt like he was in shock. Their whole marriage had unraveled in a single evening. But it was so bloodless and dead, and Maureen was so cold and without emotion or regret that it told him how far they had fallen.

He lay awake in his bed for a long time that night, trying to recall the beginning, when they loved each other, and he couldn't even remember it anymore. Even the memory of it was gone.

He called the phone numbers he had written down from his office in the morning. He had three apartments to see that afternoon. He wanted something furnished for now. He was going to leave the apartment intact for Maureen. All he wanted was some of the art, and his clothes. But he didn't want to disrupt their family home for the kids.

He didn't tell anyone where he was going when he left work. He hadn't figured out what to say to them yet, and he wanted to tell his children first.

He ran into Renee in the hall as he was leaving, and she looked at him. He looked pale and serious. "Are you okay?"

"Yeah. I'm fine. I have a headache. I think I'm coming down with a cold." She didn't believe him. He looked worse than that, but she just nodded, and he left. He had no one to talk to about it, and he didn't want to tell his parents yet and upset them. A divorce would be a big deal to them and was to him too.

By six o'clock, he had a three-bedroom furnished apartment in Tribeca in a decent building. The master bedroom looked out at the river, and it had afternoon sun. The two other bedrooms were small, but he didn't know how much time his kids would be spending with him, probably very little, but this way they could come whenever they wanted. The kitchen and bathrooms were brand-new, and the furniture was plain and inoffensive. It looked more like a fancy hotel suite than a home, but it was what he needed now. It had a small study, a dining area, and a big living room. And there was a gym with a pool in the building, which Mike thought the kids might like if they stayed with him.

The building manager explained that the owner had bought the apartment as an investment to rent, and had never lived there, which was why it seemed so impersonal. It was all he wanted now, a place to stay where no one hated him or was angry at him all the time or reminded him of past sins. It looked like a clean slate, which was all he needed. He packed that night. He took a lot of his clothes, and asked Maureen if he could take four pieces of art, paintings he had bought, and she said she didn't care. And he took some framed photos of the children from the living room, and one of him and Maureen when they were younger. She was smiling in the photograph. He hadn't seen her look like that in years.

He hired a van and driver in the morning, dropped everything off at the apartment, and then went to work. He was smiling when he walked in.

"How's your cold?" Renee asked him when she saw him. "You look a lot better today."

"I am," he said. He felt lighter. He didn't tell anyone at work. He wasn't ready to. And he booked a ticket to San Francisco for the weekend, and told Jenny he was coming out. He said he had work in San Francisco, and she said she was free for dinner on Saturday and could spend time with him in the afternoon too. He dreaded telling her, fearing she'd be upset.

It went better than he expected. They took a walk on the Stanford campus on Saturday, and they sat down on a bench under a tree. The weather was warm and it was a beautiful day.

He hesitated for a minute before he told her, and then he jumped in.

"Your mom and I made a decision," he started seriously, and she finished the sentence for him.

"You're getting a divorce," she said quietly. He searched her face to see if she was heartbroken, but she didn't look surprised or upset. He thought Maureen had told her and didn't warn him.

"Yes." He had made the decision to divorce and not just separate in the past few days. Maureen agreed. "Your mom told you?"

"No, Dad. She didn't. It's been coming for a long time. I've been expecting it since I was about fourteen. It'll be better. Can I stay with you when I come home?"

"Don't you want to stay with your mother? It's your home." He was surprised by her question.

"I can go back and forth. Mom and I fight a lot. She thinks I'm on your side, and I guess I am. She's so mean to you." And she often was to Jenny too. It struck him as sad that there were sides at all.

"I don't want to tell Zack till he comes home," he said, and Jenny nodded. She was tall with jet-black hair like his, and she had his smile and blue eyes. It was all so reasonable. "You don't have to take sides, Jen. None of this is your fault. Our marriage just died a long time ago. I wasn't home enough, for any of you."

165

"You were busy, and you were great to us when you came home. Don't let Mom tell you that you weren't. She's always mad at something or someone. She's an unhappy person. Maybe this will be good for her. She'll have to figure out her own life and stop blaming you for everything." Jenny was fair about it, and he was impressed by how mature she was and how well she had taken the news.

"I hope you like the apartment. There's a gym and a pool in the building."

"I don't care what there is or if we live in a barn. I love you, Dad." She kissed his cheek and hugged him, and he smiled with tears in his eyes. Not over what he'd lost. Over what he'd gained. It had gone so much better than he had expected. His daughter was terrific. He had always known that, and now she'd proven it to him.

Over dinner that night, Jenny asked him about what had happened with his plan to invest in Brooke's.

"It didn't work out. The owner doesn't want to give up control or sell it. I don't blame her, it's a cool place." Jennifer looked disappointed.

"I was hoping I'd get a discount. I love that store."

"Me too." He smiled at her, thinking of Spencer. He would have liked to introduce Jenny to her.

Mike and Jenny spent a nice evening together,

and he felt relieved when he left her. She was solidly on her feet and well grounded. She didn't say it, but he had the feeling she was relieved about the divorce too. It was more honest than the lie he and Maureen had been living for years, which didn't fool anyone, not even the children. He was glad he had come to tell her in person, and they had had some time together. It was always quality time with her.

He slept all the way back to New York and felt energized when he got back to the apartment. He unpacked all the clothes he had brought there and hung the four paintings Maureen had let him take. He put the photographs around the apartment, and the place looked a little more lived-in. It all still felt very new. A new chapter of his life had started. He hoped it would be a good one. He had learned from past mistakes. Now he wanted Zack to come home, so they could be a family again.

Chapter 8

Spencer continued to use the makeshift office in the basement of the store. The workmen were around all day. She checked their progress regularly, asked questions, sought out the contractor, and made constant decisions about what to keep in terms of design and what to change. It was a perfect opportunity to refresh everything.

She brought in the architect to make some changes to the restaurant and the top floor. The smell of smoke on the lower floors was gone within a week. The merchandise had been aired, and only a few things were too damaged to repair. Spencer had cleaning crews working throughout the building. Within three weeks, it looked more like a remodel than the aftermath of a fire. Spencer didn't want to go overboard, but she wanted no evidence of the trauma the store had been through to remain.

She walked around the store in overalls and working boots and a hard hat, with a clipboard, and Paul Trask followed her with a list of the estimates they'd signed and the bills they'd received. The restoration of the store was costing a fortune, but it was going to be beautiful, and Spencer was doing all she could to keep the costs down. Insurance was paying for most of it, but there was still a margin of expenses that fell into the no-man's-land between the insurance and what they had to pay for themselves, and there were a lot of those items.

Paul sat down in her office with her one day, to pursue their earlier conversations.

"We still need investment money, Spencer. The work we're doing now is costing a fortune and we're missing two months of sales, with the store closed."

"We can't open with construction still going on, someone will get injured and we'll wind up in a lawsuit."

Paul had already contacted a firm to help set up their clothing online for purchase. They had shelved the idea of an annex for now. As far as Spencer was concerned, a move was out of the question, and far too expensive. The neighborhood was dicey, but they had lived with it for this long and would continue to do so. The threat of losing control of the business entirely and selling a majority investment to someone was everything she wanted to avoid. She thought of Mike Weston occasionally and wondered how he was doing. She was sure he was making fabulous investments that were far more profitable than his investment in her store would have been. She had no remorse about turning him down. It had been the right thing for her and for the store. Paul had reminded her several times that Mike Weston had been their only option, and she reminded him each time that it had been no option at all and was the wrong one for them. It had been plain to her.

She supervised every inch of the work and pitched in occasionally. The energy she demonstrated to all inspired others to do the same. Spencer had never shirked hard work or even manual labor. She was tireless. With everyone helping, they managed to open the store a week earlier than promised, and it looked better than ever.

Mike had settled in to his apartment and Jenny was due home from her internship in July and wanted to stay with him. Maureen wasn't pleased about it, but she could hardly forbid Jenny, now twenty, to stay with her father. They had heard from Zack, and he was back in Paris. He wanted to take a short class at the Louvre, and was promising to be home by the first week in July, and he told his father that he was ready to go back to school and that as soon as he got home he'd apply for January. Mike wasn't sure how serious he was, but Zack was in good spirits and enjoying the last of his nearly yearlong odyssey. His two friends were coming home too. One of them had renewed his acceptance at NYU and would be going to school there, and the other was going to work for his father for a year while he decided what to do next.

Mike was just about to leave the office at six o'clock, earlier than usual, when he got a call on his cell phone from one of Zack's traveling partners. It was midnight in Paris, and Luke's voice was shaking. All three boys had turned nineteen while they were traveling and none of them seemed more grown up to Mike than when they left. He could tell from the sound of Luke's voice that something terrible had happened and was praying that he hadn't called to tell him that Zack was dead.

"Is Zack okay? What happened?" Mike asked. He could feel his heart pounding in his chest.

"Yes, sort of. He had a biking accident. He got hit by a bus. He's in the hospital."

"A bus?" Mike's heart pounded. "Is he conscious?"

Mike asked as he sat back down at his desk with shaking legs, fearing a brain injury.

"Yes, he's conscious," Luke assured him.

"Was he wearing a helmet?"

"No one wears them here." Mike felt sick as he listened, imagining Zack permanently impaired. "He broke a leg and both wrists, but his head is okay. We were in the bike lane, and the bus just nicked him and he fell. He's going to be okay."

"What hospital is he in?" Mike tried to gather his wits and didn't know who to call.

"I don't know, it has a weird name, like Pity Salty something. They said he could leave tomorrow, but he's going to be in a wheelchair, he can't use crutches because of his wrists." It was a nasty end to their trip, but Zack was alive, and all Mike wanted to do now was get him home in one piece. He thanked God the bus hadn't killed him and the damage wasn't worse, if what Luke said was true.

"I'll try to get a flight out tonight," Mike told him. "Where are you staying?" Luke gave him the name of a small hotel on the Left Bank.

"Greg is with him now. It just happened a few hours ago. He's all doped up and he's sleeping. We'll stay with him tonight. They said we could sleep in his room with him. We won't leave him, Mr. Weston, I promise. I think Greg and I will come home too. We'll call our parents. I'm really sorry.

Everything's been fine till now." Mike had both boys' cell phones, so he knew how to contact them.

"It's not your fault, Luke. Thank you for calling me. I'll get there as fast as I can."

He called Maureen as soon as he hung up, and she was calmer than Mike had been. Luke's quavering voice had terrified him.

"I'm going to try and catch a flight tonight. Do you want to come with me?"

"Are you going to bring him home?" she asked.

"As soon as I can."

"Then why don't I get everything organized, and you go over to get him. He should be seen by an orthopedist here as soon as possible, to be sure they set it all right." It made sense to him too, and he hoped Zack was in a decent hospital, but at least he wasn't in a coma, or dead.

He called the airline after that and got a seat on a midnight flight to Paris, with a return for both of them the night of the day he arrived. He didn't want to waste time in Paris. He just wanted to get Zack home now. And then he called the Four Seasons where he always stayed and booked a room for the day, and got the number for the emergency line at the U.S. Embassy in Paris. A clipped military voice answered immediately. He explained the situation and asked if they knew of a hospital that sounded like "Pity Salty," and if it was a decent hospital.

"That would be the Pitié-Salpêtrière, sir. It's an excellent medical facility. He'll get good care there. Is there anything we can do to help you while you're here?"

"Not that I know of, but it's good to know that I can call you." Mike was relieved that the embassy people knew the hospital and it was a good one.

"I'm sorry about your son's accident," the young marine on the line said. "I'm sure he'll be happy to see you and relieved to go home." Mike couldn't wait to get his son back to New York and have him checked out by doctors he knew.

He asked his secretary to cancel his appointments for the next few days and told her what was happening. And then he called Maureen back and told her what he was doing and where they'd be, and reassured her about the hospital.

Renee and Joe came into his office when they heard what had happened.

"Hopefully he'll be okay when I get him back here. It could have been a lot worse." And he hoped that Luke's account was accurate and that there had been no head injury. Mike wouldn't be completely reassured until he saw Zack and spoke to a doctor there. He hadn't seen his son since he'd come home for two weeks at Christmas and then went back to continue the trip. Mike was sorry now he'd let him go back. Enough was enough.

He went home to pack then. By seven-thirty, he was ready, and he didn't have to leave for the airport till nine, to check in at ten for the midnight flight. He lay down on his bed for a minute to unwind and try to calm down after hearing what had happened. He had never been as frightened in his life as when he answered Luke's call. He realized now that Luke must have been crying. It must have been terrifying for him and Greg too. It was definitely time for the boys to come home. And he was grateful that Maureen was being calm. She already had an appointment for Zack with an orthopedist the day after their return.

Mike was lying on his bed thinking about all of it, and he didn't even know why, but he wanted to call Spencer. There was no one he could talk to. Maureen had been sensible and efficient—she had always been good in a crisis and had handled many of them—but there was nothing warm and comforting about her, and all he wanted now was to hear the sound of Spencer's voice, which seemed crazy even to him. He hardly knew her. He still had her cell phone number in his phone, and he gave in to the impulse and called her.

She answered as soon as she saw his name come up, sounding surprised.

"Hi, Mike, how are you?" she asked in her pleasant voice. She sounded happy to hear him.

"I'm sorry to call you. I just wanted to talk to you for a minute. It's not about business. I'm leaving for Paris tonight. I got a call two hours ago that my son was in a biking accident. He was hit by a bus, and it could have been a lot worse. He broke a leg and both wrists, but if that's all it is, he's damn lucky. He wasn't even wearing a helmet. His friend says they don't wear them in France."

"That's true, they don't," Spencer confirmed. "Or at least they didn't the last time I was there. I'm so sorry. You must have been frantic when you heard. If I can do anything to help when he gets back, let me know." He could hear her sons playing in the background, shouting and laughing.

"It sounds lively at your house," he said, smiling.

"It's crazy hour before they go to bed," she explained.

"How's the restoration coming at the store?"

"We're almost finished. They did it sooner than expected. It's looking good."

"I'm happy to hear it." There was something so soothing about her voice. He felt a little foolish calling her, but he was glad he had. "Everything else all right with you?"

"Yeah, just working on the store day and night to get it open again." She sounded happy and relaxed.

"My daughter was very disappointed we didn't

make a deal. She wanted a big discount." Spencer laughed at what he said.

"Tell her to come in and see me. I'll see what I can do."

"I'll bring her in when she comes home. I went out to San Francisco to see her a few weeks ago. She has an internship out there and then she'll be home for a month or six weeks before she goes back to school." He wondered if Maureen would take them to Maine this summer without him. She had no summer plans so far, with everything changed between them. And he doubted that Zack would be able to go sailing now.

"Thank you for calling to tell me what happened to your son. Let me know if I can do anything," she reminded him.

"He's going to be very hampered with both wrists broken, so he can't use crutches for the broken leg. It's going to be a full-time job taking care of him. I'm just grateful it wasn't worse. I nearly had a heart attack when his friend called. I called the embassy and they said he's in an excellent hospital. I'll feel better when I see him, but for now I'm feeling very lucky."

"I'll think good thoughts for you both tonight," she reassured him, and it made him glad he had called her. She was the kind of woman who always seemed to have words of comfort. He had sensed that about her. "Try and sleep on the flight. It's a short flight to Paris, only six hours, and you'll have your hands full when you get there. Is anyone going with you to help you?" she asked, concerned.

"No, his friends can help me in Paris, and we're flying back tomorrow night. His mother is organizing things here. He's going to be a lot for her to manage. He's a big guy." Mike didn't explain that he was no longer living with Maureen. It didn't even occur to him to say it, but she thought that what he'd said was odd, and didn't want to pry. He had called her, that was enough. Maybe he meant that his son would be a lot to manage in the daytime while Mike was at work. She had thought of Mike several times since she'd last seen him, when she'd rejected the deal he had offered her. She had wondered if he was angry at her, but he didn't sound it.

"Can I call you when you get back?" she asked him. "Just to find out how he is."

"Of course. I'll give you a full report. And Spencer, thanks for being there and listening."

"No worries, Mike. I'm always here if you need to talk." It was more than he'd had from Maureen in the past ten years.

It was eight o'clock by then, and he lay on his bed for another hour thinking about Spencer before he left for the airport. He checked in and went to the first-class lounge and helped himself to some snacks, still thinking about his conversation with Spencer. It had been nice to hear her voice and find out that things were going well with the renovation.

Mike boarded the flight and ate a light meal before going to sleep for the rest of the flight. The steward woke him with croissants and coffee right before they landed at Charles de Gaulle Airport. The flight was on time and it was noon in Paris. The car and driver his secretary had hired were waiting for him, and drove him straight to the hospital. The staff at the information desk spoke English, and they gave him directions to the ward where Zack's room was. He found it easily a few minutes later, knocked on the door, and found Zack sitting up in bed with a grazed cheek and a black eye, both wrists in short casts, his leg in a cumbersome cast, and a wheelchair at the foot of the bed. Luke and Greg looked relieved to see him, and Zack looked sheepish, but there were tears in his eyes when his father approached the bed and leaned down to kiss him.

"Training for the Tour de France, were you?" he said with a rueful smile, and Zack laughed, relieved that his father wasn't angry. The doctor came to check on him a few minutes later. He told Mike essentially the same things the boys had reported to him. Hc said that it had been a clean break, but Zack would have to wear the cast on his leg for eight weeks, which would hamper him for most of the summer. The wrists would heal more quickly. The doctor reiterated that Zack had been incredibly lucky. He could easily have been killed by the bus, and he admitted to his father that he had drifted slightly out of the bike lane, that the bus had not slipped into the bike lane. The accident had been Zack's fault.

The hospital discharged Zack shortly after Mike got there, and they all went to a suite at the Four Seasons for the day. Before they left the hospital, Mike called Maureen, and handed the phone to Zack so he could talk to his mother. With the broken wrists, he couldn't do anything for himself.

They ordered room service at the hotel, and the other boys went to get Zack's things from their hotel and bring them to the Four Seasons. He was traveling very light, with everything in his backpack. Greg and Luke were staying two more days, and then they would be home too. Their year of trekking around Europe was over. Mike was relieved.

Mike and Zack were on an eight o'clock flight that night back to New York that was due to land in New York at nine-thirty P.M. local time. Mike had told Maureen he'd have Zack home to her around ten-thirty or eleven, and she said she was ready for him. It was going to be hard managing him with a broken leg and two broken wrists.

Mike wasn't sure of the timing, so soon after the accident, but he told Zack on the plane that he and Maureen were separated. Zack would know as soon as Mike left the apartment to go back to his own place, so he had to tell him. Zack looked sad but not surprised. It had been obvious for years that his parents didn't get along and had deteriorated into a loveless marriage.

"Are you getting divorced?" Zack asked him.

"It looks that way," Mike told him calmly, and then Zack surprised him.

"Can I stay with you, Dad?" he asked.

"Don't you want to stay at your mom's and sleep in your own bed?"

Zack shook his head.

"I'd rather stay with you, and I can't even go to the bathroom by myself without help." There was a practical side to it now that Mike hadn't thought of. "But I'd want to stay with you anyway," he added and smiled shyly at his father. "I want to see your new apartment. Do you have room for me?" He looked worried.

"Of course, and there's a gym and a pool, for when you're feeling better." Zack looked excited to be with him, so for all Maureen's claims that

Mike had ruined his relationship with him forever, there was no sign of it. Zack was happy to be with his dad. Maureen wanted Mike to think his kids hated him.

Mike had had his secretary order a wheelchair for Zack that was supposed to be in the car when the driver picked them up in New York. He was going to have to explain to Maureen that Zack wanted to stay with him. He decided to use Zack's bathroom needs as the excuse, but he suspected she would be disappointed anyway. But Mike was going to drop him off to her in the daytime. He would need a lot of help for a while, and some tender loving care. Mike's mind raced ahead to the thought of hiring a helper of some kind at home for Zack while he was at the office every day.

Mike had texted Maureen right before the flight took off, to assure her that everything was on track and in order, and the flight was on time. And then he had texted Spencer. "About to take off. All well in Paris. The young eagle is in surprisingly good shape all things considered. Talk soon. Best, Mike."

He settled back to have dinner with Zack on the luxurious first-class flight. Zack looked right at home. After having backpacked around Europe for eight months, Zack was ready to come home and be pampered for a while, and Mike was excited that his son would be staying with him. He may have missed out when Zack was a little kid, but in spite of all of Maureen's dire predictions, he wasn't missing out now, and Zack had forgiven him his earlier absences and loved being with him. Mike felt like a lucky man as he watched his son sleep on the flight, and thanked God again that Zack was alive.

Chapter 9

The orthopedist Maureen took Zack to looked over his X-rays and was satisfied with the way the bones had been set. He told him what they all already knew, that Zack was lucky to be alive. It was a miracle the bus hadn't killed him when Zack drifted out of the bike lane. The driver didn't even see him until he was on the ground, and people were screaming to warn the driver. All Zack could do now was wait until the bones healed. He was going to be very hampered in the meantime, particularly with both wrists in casts.

Mike and Maureen organized a babysitting system for him. Mike dropped him off at his mother's on the way to work, and picked him up on the way home at night. That way Zack got to spend time with both his parents, who had missed him for so long, and he was enjoying having his father to himself at night in Mike's new apartment. Maureen knew a college student looking for odd jobs who had agreed to come to her house in the daytime to help them out. Zack settled in quickly and felt at home in the new apartment. Once Greg and Luke were back in New York, they often came over in the evenings, sometimes with other friends, and hung out with him, while Mike ordered food for them, and let them spend time together without interfering. When he did join them, they told him about their adventures on the trip. For the most part, it sounded like wholesome good fun, with a few scary episodes that had added some spice to their long trip and had proven to be harmless in the end, except for the final chapter with the bus.

Spencer sent Mike an occasional text to ask how Zack was doing, and it sounded as though they were managing very well. During his second week home, Zack had sent in his applications to NYU, Eugene Lang College, and Columbia for admission in January. He rejected Mike's suggestion of MIT. Having been away for a year, he wanted to stay in New York, and Mike didn't object. He was happy to have his son home, although he'd be living in the dorms once he started school.

* * *

When the store reopened, Spencer was busier than ever, and she noticed that the homeless population in the neighborhood seemed to have increased. While the construction was in progress, there had been nooks and crannies where they could set up their "cribs," as the homeless called them, and their tents, and there was garbage near the entrance to the store every morning, rolled-up sleeping bags in doorways, and shopping carts full of belongings along the sidewalk. Spencer's customers commented on it, and she was trying to figure out ways to help the homeless while keeping them at a distance from the store. One morning one of them, who had become a familiar face in the neighborhood, was standing a few feet from the entrance, stark naked, giving himself a shower from a hose, and she didn't want to call the police. The doorman had escorted him rapidly away, but it was an ongoing problem she was eager to solve.

She finally had an idea late one night. In the morning, she spoke to Paul Trask about it and asked for his help.

"I need some kind of space to rent, with a large interior area, like an old garage, a warehouse, an art gallery. I need one big room. It doesn't need to be habitable or pretty or chic, but it has to be big, about ten blocks from the store. It's going to be a work and storage space, not a store," she explained. "And we need a bathroom."

"Is this for our annex?" Paul's eyes lit up at the prospect, and Spencer shook her head.

"It's not our annex. This is for something else. I'm not ready for our annex yet." She didn't explain further. The insurance had paid for a good part of the repairs and renovations after the fire, but not all of it, so it was an added, unexpected expense. She didn't want to incur more big expenses at the moment, but if done right, the project she had in mind shouldn't cost too much. After that, she spoke to HR, and asked them to put up a notice asking people to sign up if they wanted to make some extra money working late on a special project. She was going to pay them, and also the rent for the location, out of her own pocket. She assumed she would get mostly the young employees who might sign up. She was planning to pay minimum wage, and didn't want to pay more. They had about fifteen names at the end of a week. And two weeks after Spencer had asked him, Paul Trask walked into her office with some photographs.

"I don't know what you want it for, Spencer, but I think I might have found what you're looking for. It's an old brick garage. A car mechanic rented it for thirty years. He retired, and it's standing empty.

It's ten blocks from here. It's no thing of beauty, but it's functional, and it's big, and it has a basic bathroom."

"It sounds perfect. When can I see it?" She smiled at him. "Is it expensive?"

"No, it's cheap. It's been standing vacant for two years. Now are you going to tell me what you're up to?"

"Soon," she promised him. She made a date to see it with him that afternoon. She was thrilled when she saw it. It was exactly what she had in mind. And now she had to do the rest. She'd been refining the concept in her head for weeks, and was excited about it. She hadn't told a soul what she was up to.

She asked Marcy to place an order for a hundred down jackets at wholesale prices, in four sizes—medium, large, extra-large, and a small, average size for women—a hundred sleeping bags, gloves, beanies, blankets, sweatshirts, T-shirts and big white cotton shirts for summer, insulated tarps, some collapsible umbrellas, small tool kits, hygiene supplies, nonperishable food snacks, and staples like instant coffee, tea bags, and sugar.

"This isn't for Brooke's," she explained to Marcy, "it's for me to give away. I want solid quality that won't fall apart in your hands, at the best prices we can get. This is an experiment. And I need big

189

cheap tote bags to put it all in, one for each person. And a bottle they can carry water in." Marcy was intrigued, and so was Paul Trask. Spencer signed a six-month lease for the garage at a ridiculously low price. It needed some repairs but not for what they were doing, and it had an alarm to protect it. And an iron gate in front, and the bathroom worked, for the employees who would be there.

"What are you going to do with all this stuff?" Marcy asked her. "Who's it for?" She was intrigued.

"You'll see," Spencer said mysteriously.

"When do you need it?"

"As soon as you can get it."

Within a week, everything had arrived, and she had it put in the garage, after she had the place thoroughly cleaned by the store's janitorial staff, working at night. She had Paul buy her some old collapsible card tables, and they bought a few long ones secondhand.

Spencer sent emails to the fifteen employees who were interested in extra work at night and asked them to come to the garage a few days later, after the store closed. She was there herself before they arrived. Marcy and Beau had volunteered to come with her for her mystery project. She had spread the supplies out on the tables herself before the employees showed up. She explained the principle of it when they got there. She wanted to load

190

the tote bags they'd gotten with one of everything, a jacket, a sweatshirt, a pack of T-shirts, socks, sleeping bag, food, tools, basic hygiene supplies, all of it.

"I want us to pack the bags, and we're going to leave the bags here, as neatly as we can. We're going to put these signs on the windows of the store." Spencer had made big red hearts herself, and on each of them, it said "We want to help. If you need supplies (brand-new jackets, sleeping bags, etc.) come to (the address of the garage), every Tuesday after work hours." And underneath it, in bold, "Please don't camp here at night." "It's a trade-off," she explained to Marcy and Beau. "Don't camp in front of the store, and we'll give you great new stuff for free. And we found a spot that's just far enough away, so I hope that out of respect, they won't come back to the store to camp, and they'll stick around where 'their own store' is."

"Oh my God, Spence, you're a genius," Beau said. "It's a brilliant idea. If it works, we'll be giving them great supplies, and keeping them away from our customers. Everybody wins. It's like the lottery for everyone, and they're all winners."

Spencer explained the plan in detail to the fifteen employees who had shown up. Half a dozen of them could man the tables with the supplies. The others could walk past with the bags and fill them.

"We'll pile them up here and one night a week, Tuesday or another day, we'll hand out the bags. We can open on other nights if we want to."

"You want to do this once a week?" Marcy asked her. "It's going to cost you."

"I know. But someone has to help the homeless. It breaks my heart to see them on the street. And if they do us the courtesy of not camping in front of the store, our customers will be happy too, and so will we. I don't want people afraid to come here because they think the neighborhood is dangerous. It isn't, but it looks that way at times. I've been trying to think of what we can do to help the homeless. No one is doing anything for them. It's time we did. And I'm hoping they stay closer to the garage at night, rather than setting up camp in front of our windows. If they don't camp at the store, it will be a bonus for us."

"It'll be good publicity for the store," Paul commented, always with his eye on benefits to Brooke's.

"That's not the point. But maybe it will set an example for others to help them too. If every business in the area reached out to help all these people, they'd be better off than they are now. Everyone wants to turn a blind eye and let someone else help them. I want to be the someone else. I thought about starting a soup kitchen, but it's too complicated. You need a lot of permits to serve food, food spoils, and you lose a big percentage. Tarps and sleeping bags don't go bad, and you don't need a permit to give them away. Maybe no one will show up, but let's try it and see what happens."

Two of the female employees looked nervous after Spencer described her plan and spoke up.

"What if they attack us, and someone gets hurt, or they rob us?" one of them asked Spencer.

"I hope that won't happen. But you should only do it if you want to. There are no points for doing it, and no black marks against you if you don't. This isn't part of your job at Brooke's, it's an experiment I want to try. We may find out that it doesn't work, or that no one comes. It's just a drop in the ocean of what they need, but if we can ease their pain a little, then it's a good thing to do. But only do it if you want to."

Marcy was smiling as she listened to Spencer speak to the group standing in the garage. She was thinking how proud Thornton would have been of her. He had had a strong sense of community too, not just commerce. He had a big heart, just like his granddaughter.

"Your Grampa would be very proud of you," Marcy whispered to her, and Spencer smiled. She pointed to the coffee machine she had bought, and promised that there would be doughnuts, fruit, coffee, and sodas on the nights they worked there.

"How late will we stay open?" a young man asked, whom Spencer recognized from designer shoes. He was wearing torn jeans and high-top Converse for his off hours. Each employee had a locker at the store where they left their uniform clothes.

"As late as we have customers," Spencer answered. "You can leave whenever you need to. We'll need a night or two to load the bags. And a night or more to hand them out. I have no idea how many people will show up. This is all new to me too."

They stayed to chat for another hour, and agreed to load the bags on Monday. And they planned to hand them out on Tuesday. Only one young man dropped out. He said he was afraid to catch an illness from being in close contact with the homeless people. He said it quietly to Spencer before he left, and she smiled and said that was fine. The other fourteen were excited about the plan. They were all chattering animatedly when they left, and Spencer was left with Marcy, Beau, and Paul, as she turned off the lights and locked up, and closed the iron gate.

"This could turn into a bigger project than you expect it to," Paul warned her, always the voice of reason and caution in their midst.

"We'll just do what we can," she said, with a peaceful look. What they were planning to do made her happy. Her only regret so far was not having thought of it before. People living on the streets weren't new in the neighborhood, but there were so many of them now, you couldn't avoid them, or avoid wanting to do something about it, other than calling the police to chase them away.

"I wonder if they'll stay away from the store now at night," Beau said as they left the garage.

"It would be good for the store if they do," Spencer said. "Our customers are upset about them. And Joel spends a lot of time moving them on in the morning." He was the doorman. "We'll have to see how it all shakes out."

"What are you going to call it?" Marcy asked her, as they walked down the street together. She had already said she wanted to help pack the bags, and was familiar with the merchandise since she had ordered it. She had even ordered the tote bags, not knowing what they were for, and was glad she had bought big, strong ones.

"Do we need a name?" Spencer looked surprised. "We shouldn't tie it to the store. I don't want to create any liability for Brooke's." Paul looked relieved when she said it, and he was wondering if they should get releases from the people who agreed to work at the garage just in case something bad happened. Many of the people on the streets were on drugs or mentally ill or both, and were unpredictable. "What about 'Free Love'?" Spencer suggested, and they all smiled. "It kind of says what it's about."

They left each other at the corner. Marcy and Paul headed for the subway to go uptown, and Beau took an Uber to Tribeca and dropped Spencer off at her place.

"You're a busy little bee, Ms. Brooke. One minute you're all dolled up, looking like a goddess of glamour at the Met, and the next minute you're handing out free supplies from a falling-down old garage. There's no telling what you'll get up to next." She smiled at him as she settled back in the Uber.

"It just seems like the right thing to do, doesn't it?" He nodded and gave her a hug when they stopped at her house. It was late, and she knew the boys would already be in bed. She had told Francine she'd be home later than usual, so not to keep them up. She hated missing an evening with them, but it was for a good cause. One day, when they were older, she wanted to teach them to reach out to less fortunate people too.

"You should sleep well tonight," Beau told her. "You're doing a beautiful thing for these people." He knew that was who she was, a woman with a big heart. He was sorry she didn't have a good man in her life to help her and appreciate her. He had never been impressed by Bill Kelly, who was a zero in Beau's book. But he wondered if Spencer would have had time to think of projects like this one if she had a man in her life. Maybe not. She had thought about that too. She had the store and her boys, maybe that was enough. None of the men in her life had ever turned out to be worthwhile. Selfish, spoiled, narcissistic. They'd been more interested in themselves and what they could get out of her than in building a real life with her. Bart wasn't even a good father. He spent more time with his ex-debutante girlfriend than with his sons. Her own father hadn't been much of a warmhearted human being either. Just a lazy guy who never pushed himself hard, coasted on his own father's accomplishments, and had a spoiled wife who didn't have a kind word to say about anyone, even her own daughter. Spencer combined the energy and forward-thinking brilliance of her grandfather, and his big heart, with the style and spirit and kindness of her grandmother. It was a winning combination, and she hoped her sons would turn out to be like their great-grandparents too. There were so many things she wanted to teach her sons, so many traditions and life lessons she wanted to share with them as they grew up, as her grandparents had done with her.

* * *

At the meeting at the garage, Spencer had made a point of saying that she didn't want to publicize their project for the homeless. It would be self-serving to do that, and look as though she was trying to find gimmicks to enhance the image of the store. It wasn't about that. But she wasn't going to hide it either. She just wanted to do it, and not waste time talking about it. But as always in the small, enclosed world of the store, there was always gossip, and her mother called her that weekend. One of the old secretaries had told Eileen about the project. She used them to gather rumors instead of asking her daughter for facts, or showing interest in what she did.

"I hear you're collecting old clothes for the homeless and going to hand them out in front of the store," her mother said in a disapproving tone when she called her, and Spencer laughed at how distorted the rumor had gotten.

"No, I'm buying new clothes, and planning to give them away out of a garage I rented for that purpose. We're overrun with homeless these days. They're camped out all over the neighborhood. And they like doing it in front of the store because it's well lit and safe."

"They've been doing that for years," her mother said dismissively, as though it weren't really a problem. "Why don't you just call the police? That's what your father did to get rid of them." It didn't surprise Spencer to hear it.

"I'd like to help them if I can, and encourage them not to just set up camp in front of the store. I didn't know that Dad used to call the cops to chase them off."

"Sometimes he gave them a little extra cash to send them away if he saw them inside himself. It always worked."

"For whom?" Spencer said.

"For the store of course. You don't want those filthy people hanging around." The way her mother described them made Spencer's heart ache, but it didn't surprise her about her mother, nothing did. The milk of human kindness did not run thick in her veins.

"So, what's new with you, Mother?" The question usually unleashed a litany of complaints, followed by some new physical problem Eileen was cultivating.

"My gout is killing me."

"You can control it with diet." With a little self-restraint. Her mother loved rich foods.

"So why are you giving things out to the homeless? You'll get fleas and lice, you know. Or TB." Eileen came back to her original subject with a vengeance. "You're not letting them into the store, are you, or feeding them?"

"No, you need permits for that. We're going to give them clothes and some supplies they need."

"You'll just encourage them to stay on the streets." It was a familiar mantra Spencer had heard before, which made no sense. No one was going to stay on the streets, in miserable conditions, for free socks and a sleeping bag and a jacket. The project was about arming them for survival, not seducing them into homelessness. The very idea was ridiculous.

"I don't think that's the issue, Mom," Spencer said simply, and moved on. "It's good to do something for the community." And the human race. "Do you want to come and see the boys? You haven't seen them in a while." Spencer hated her mother's visits but felt duty-bound to ask her. She was their only grandparent, but hardly ever saw them. She was more involved in herself.

"They always have runny noses or stomach flu. I don't want to catch anything from them. They're little disease factories at that age." It was one way to look at it. It always startled Spencer how little desire her mother had to see the twins. She didn't consider them "interesting" yet, at seven. Eileen had felt that way about Spencer too, and by the time she did find her daughter interesting, Spencer had left for college, and they never connected except at a dutiful, superficial level on Spencer's part. Her mother wasn't a warm person, and Spencer found it impossible to relate to her. They were just too different. Her mother considered their differences a fatal flaw in her daughter, and never questioned herself, nor sought to improve their relationship. Spencer had given up on having a real relationship with her long ago. Her grandparents had given her all the love she needed. Her parents had both been selfish and cold. And Spencer's relationship with her boys was intentionally the opposite, warm, open, and loving. She spent all her spare time with them. "I might come to lunch at the store one of these days," Eileen conceded. "I want to see what the renovations look like since the fire." Spencer knew she'd be looking for mistakes to criticize.

"They did a very nice job," Spencer said. "It's even prettier than before."

"That's not what I hear." Spencer could just envision Eileen's expression when she said it, with pursed lips. It was the facial expression Spencer always associated with her mother, as much as she did her grandmother's shy flirtatious smile, and her grandfather's laughing eyes, and her father's stern expression of long-suffering disapproval. Like many families, hers was a mixed bag. The good genes had skipped a generation.

* * *

The first night of packing in the garage was predictably chaotic. No one knew exactly what they were doing, since they hadn't done it before. They were learning as they went along. Marcy and Beau were on the team to pack the bags. Spencer walked from group to group, seeing how it all fit together, and tried packing one of the bags herself, to find the best system. It all worked, and what they were giving people would keep them warm in winter, cool in summer weather, covered, dry, and lightly fed. They gave them what they needed to sleep, for rain, utensils to eat with, what they could use to get clean, and even a deck of cards. It was a survival kit for the streets.

They ran out of a few items, which Marcy replaced, flashlights and batteries, and they needed more socks. With eighteen of them doing it, since everyone had showed up—fourteen employees, three department heads, and Spencer herself—they packed all hundred bags in one night and had scheduled their "Opening Night" for the following day, after work.

Spencer had made the big heart-shaped red signs, which she was going to tape inside the store windows the next day and leave them there. Big beautiful red hearts, with glitter letters that said, "Free Love," and all the pertinent information for the garage below them, and at the bottom in smaller but noticeable black letters, the gentle request not to camp in front of the store at night. She wondered if it would work. Whether it did or not, the local homeless would get supplies they needed desperately.

They were all excited when they left that night. It felt like the eve of opening night of a big event. They were looking forward to it and planned to be there the next night to hand the bags out. Spencer and Beau high-fived each other, as Marcy looked on, smiling broadly, after Spencer taped the signs inside the windows, for all to see as they walked past the following afternoon. She saw people stop and read them and hoped the homeless population would too.

Their first "customer" peered into the big open doors of the garage the following evening around eight o'clock. Spencer and her team had had a nervous hour waiting, eating doughnuts Spencer had brought with her. It was a balmy evening, and she and her staff looked at each other, wondering if anyone would come. Maybe no one would show up. And then they began to come one by one, curious as they looked inside, suspicious at first, some frightened, greeted by the welcoming, smiling faces of the people who had packed the bags the night before. Marcy had already placed orders for the next batch of supplies. It wasn't cheap, but it was how Spencer wanted to spend her money, and Marcy heartily approved and tried to get the best deals she could.

By nine o'clock, there were about forty people milling around inside the garage. Only two were women, and the staff had set bags aside for them, with the smaller-sized jackets and socks. It was all unisex, except for the sizing of a few items. The recipients wanted to know why the workers were doing it, where the supplies had come from, were they from a church, was it a gift from Brooke's? Spencer wanted no credit for it, and not to be singled out. The staff reminded each recipient, with a gentle request, not to camp out for the night in front of the store anymore, and they promised to pass the message on. The people who left with the bags thanked their benefactors profusely, hugged some of them, and left to discover what was inside. Some crouched on the floor to take their bags apart right there, and exclaimed at what was in them, and put some things on immediately, or opened a bag of cookies and ate one.

By eleven o'clock, the team had given away seventy-one bags and had enough left for people to come back the next night for a few hours to hand them out. Most of the team were willing to do so.

A few had other plans. They hugged each other as their last "customer" of the night left. They all agreed the evening had been a roaring success. They all felt great about it. The faces of the grateful recipients were unforgettable.

Spencer took an Uber home, and had the driver go past the store. There was only one man in a sleeping bag lying in front of one of the windows, where an air vent would keep him warm. And the sleeping bag wasn't one of those they had given out, so he hadn't heard the word, although he could see the sign in the window.

Spencer had tears in her eyes as she rode home. She could hear her grandfather's voice in her head. "Good girl!" It was one of those precious moments in a lifetime when all the ugliness faded and she knew who she was, and that she was doing the right thing. It made her feel like she had wings and could fly. She kissed Ben and Axel asleep in their beds when she got home, just wanting to share the love with them.

Chapter 10

Mike was learning a lot about parenting from living with Zack when he came home from Europe badly injured. Zack wasn't in pain most of the time, except if he overdid it, but he got petulant and frustrated from being confined to the wheelchair, because he couldn't use crutches with his broken wrists. Mike was learning about his son's maturity level and his more open-minded view of the world than his father's, which were astonishing at times. And so were his total lack of maturity and insight at other times, when Mike thought he acted like a five-year-old. In fact, they were learning a lot about each other, and filling in the years they had missed. What had been terrifying at first had turned into an amazing opportunity to bridge the gap between them and make up for lost time. It annoyed Maureen to see how close Mike and Zack were becoming, she didn't think Mike deserved a second chance. But a better part of her realized that it was what their son needed, to get to know his father and have a male role model to teach him how to become a man.

Zack was shocked to discover how conservative his father's political views were, but Mike viewed the world through the eyes of a self-made man, a very rich one, and endorsed policies that would protect what he had built and the wealth he had acquired, which Zack vehemently disapproved of. They had heated political discussions late into the night, and even though their points of view differed, Mike welcomed the exchange, and encouraged Zack to support his own opinions. He didn't expect Zack to share his point of view at nineteen, and would have been surprised if he did.

Mike said something about it one day to Maureen when he came to pick Zack up, and how proud he was of their son. Her reaction was bittersweet, but deep down, she was happy for Zack. He needed a father, even if Mike had woken up to it late in the day. And Mike was grateful for the opportunity to have the chance to be one, even if they had been nearly strangers until now. Zack was being generous with his trust and his time, and opening up to his father as he hadn't before.

It worried Maureen that Zack would need her less now, and love her less, and Mike understood and reassured her. "You'll always be his mom, Maureen. He needs us both." She nodded, with tears in her eyes, and she missed Zack at night when he slept at Mike's apartment, but it worked better for Zack, needing Mike's help to shower, use the bathroom, and get into bed, with his casts. And the arrangement they had was working. The college student Maureen had hired was helpful in the daytime. Mike was strong and in good shape and he could manage to help Zack at night, although Zack was bigger than he was, and had shot up and filled out during his time in Europe.

His friends were being faithful about visiting him, and there was a girl from his high school senior year whom he was in touch with and wanted to take out when he could manage and get around on his own again. She came to see him once at Mike's apartment, and they played video games, and Mike ordered dinner for them and stayed in his small study to leave them alone. Zack had gotten used to his independence and freedom while traveling in Europe, and it was hard to be treated like a child by his parents when he got back. But his injuries had created that situation, so he tried to be understanding about their being overprotective and worrying about him. Zack hated being an invalid for the summer.

Their summer plans were on hold for the moment. Mike had wanted to rent a house in the Hamptons for a few weeks when Jennifer was home, but hadn't found one yet. And Maureen had planned to go to Italy with friends while Zack and Jennifer were with Mike, but she wanted to wait and see how Zack was doing by then. Nothing was definite yet. Zack wouldn't be able to manage the beach, or swim in the ocean with his leg in a cast, so he had told Mike he might spend time in the city too.

So far Zack had been a pleasure, not a burden, and Mike wasn't dating anyone, so he didn't interfere with Mike's private life. Mike hadn't dated anyone since he and Maureen had split up, although Zack hinted that his mother had, but he offered no details. He didn't want to get in the middle between them. They were all still getting used to the idea of the divorce. But Maureen had moved on faster than Mike. He wasn't surprised. She hadn't loved him for years.

Zack had talked to his sister about it, and she said she had been expecting the divorce for years, and thought their parents would be happier now. Zack didn't disagree, but he didn't like the idea of having divorced parents, and he worried about who they'd get involved with now, bad boyfriends or girlfriends, people with their own kids, or who'd want to change everything, or come between them and their parents. He was just getting to know his father and he didn't want to lose him.

"You won't," Jenny reassured him. "Dad's not like that, unless he hooks up with a real loser. He may not have been around much, but he loves us a lot." She was even more sure of that than her brother, who had listened to their mother say bad things about him for years and believed a lot of it. Zack realized now that many of the things Maureen said weren't true. Their mother had her own issues with Mike, which Zack could see more clearly now. He could see too that their father was worthy of more respect than he'd been shown by Maureen, who had painted him black to his children for years.

Mike hadn't told the kids yet, but he had informed Maureen that he had called his lawyer and started the ball rolling for their divorce. He had finally given up on their marriage, after too many years hoping it would change. He saw now that it couldn't have. Too much had gone wrong for too long, and Maureen was never going to forgive him for his failures in their marriage. But with luck, their children would. Jenny had always been understanding and had her own problems with their mother. Zack was coming to it more slowly, but was on the right path, just from getting to know his father and living with him now. The apartment was small, but big enough for them, living like two bachelors, side by side, father and son. Mike let him have a beer from time to time, and they talked like two men sharing an apartment. Zack liked it when his father treated him like an adult. Maureen coddled and babied him, especially now with his injuries. He used to love it, but it got on his nerves now. He wanted to be treated like a man, even though he was only halfway there. Mike understood that and treated him accordingly. He had felt the same way at Zack's age. He had thought he was an adult when he left for college. Zack had grown up a lot during his gap year in Europe, and Mike could see now the benefits it had offered Zack. He would have grown up much more slowly at home. And he had needed to get away from the constant war between his parents. Now the war was over. And in peacetime, they were thriving and growing. And Mike's relationship with his kids was solid.

Spencer was having her own struggles with her sons. Ben was learning to read more slowly than Axel, and not doing as well in school, although he was a happy child. Axel worked harder in his studies with good results. He read easily, but he was quieter and more withdrawn. She thought the differences might be related to their being twins. The school called her, and wanted her to get an assessment of Ben's abilities, and a psychological evaluation. There were occasional disciplinary problems with both boys, and the school counselor commented that both boys said they hardly ever saw their father, and they didn't like his girlfriend. They had told the counselor that their mom worked all the time at her job, that she stayed late a lot of the time, and came home when they were already in bed. With some exaggeration, they said they only saw her on Sundays, even though she had dinner with them several times a week. She always tried to come home as early as she could, but problems often came up that she had to stay and handle, and she thought their Saturday nights and full days on Sunday compensated for it. The school counselor didn't agree and sounded critical of her. Her comments went straight to Spencer's heart, like a scalpel of guilt.

"What do other parents do who work?" Spencer said, irritated by the counselor's supercilious attitude when she went to the school to see her. She felt slightly betrayed by her sons. "What about doctors or lawyers? What do they do? I try to have dinner with the boys every night I can, but sometimes it's just not possible." Sometimes she was at the store till eight, dealing with a crisis. And now, with her new Free Love project, she was out at least two nights a week till late, sometimes three.

The Free Love project was a startling success. It hadn't fully solved the problem of homeless people camping out in front of the store, but had reduced it considerably, and even more importantly, the team was reaching out to a segment of the population who were getting too little help from government agencies and none from private citizens. They couldn't cure the problem and stop homelessness, but they were making a difference at a grassroots level. But was Spencer sacrificing her sons for them? She didn't want that to happen. It was hard to do everything she had to do and meet all her parental obligations too. Everywhere she turned, all the responsibilities were on her shoulders, with no one to share them, and now the twins were showing signs that she wasn't adequately providing emotionally for them. She felt like a failure. It was hard to feel like a success on every front, and sometimes on any front at all. Some part of her life was always falling through the cracks, no matter how hard she tried. The boys were the most important part of her life, and that part needed to go smoothly and be tucked up first, not last. She felt like a terrible mother as she listened to the counselor explain just how she was failing her sons. It was hard to get it all right, although God knew she tried. But trying didn't count if she didn't get it right, and the boys weren't getting what they needed from her. Francine, although superbly competent with meals and bath time, was just a nanny and not their mother. It sounded to Spencer as though she was getting a failing grade in mothering. And she always hated hearing people say they "did their best" if they got poor results. It was no excuse.

"Let's talk about some counseling for both boys after we get the evaluation on Ben. Axel is doing well in school, although I'd like to see him more outgoing, and less dependent on his brother," the counselor said. "Is there anything you can do about their seeing more of their father? That seems to be upsetting them too," she went on imperiously. Clearly, she was a woman who felt she had never fallen short on any subject, and believed that she was perfect. The oracle from God. She made Spencer feel like an utter disaster, and deeply humiliated. She was getting low marks in the most important part of her life, her children.

"No, there really is nothing I can do about their father," Spencer said, sounding exasperated. "I've tried. We got divorced when they were very young, and he's never been very involved, nor very interested. There's nothing I can do about it."

"And there are no other male figures in their lives? Family, uncles, grandfathers?" Nope, blew it again, Spencer thought. She had no boyfriend, no brothers, no male role models for them.

"I'm afraid not. And I can't trade them for a pair of girls." She was annoyed at the counselor. "We're doing the best we can with what we've got." It sounded like a lame excuse to Spencer.

"I'm sure you're trying, Ms. Brooke. We just need to get better results. We'll see what the evaluation says about how Ben is doing." And then what? They fire her as a mother? What more could one do when one's best was not enough? How did one ever give children all they needed, when life pulled you in a thousand directions all at once?

Spencer's mother helped to reinforce Spencer's sense of inadequacy. She pointed to everything she thought Spencer was doing wrong, and never to her successes. She thought that Spencer's Free Love program was a ridiculous waste of time, money, and energy, and she couldn't understand why Spencer would do it, since compassion for others and generosity to the less fortunate were not on her radar.

The only thing that cheered Spencer and reassured her that she was on the right path was working one-on-one with the homeless on the nights she did. It touched her deeply every time and added a profound joy, peace, and satisfaction to her life. And she was encouraged when they got Ben's test results. He had a slight delay in reading ability but the educational psychologist found him to be happy and well-adjusted, so maybe Spencer was doing better than she feared, despite the school counselor's initial critical appraisal. She had just assumed that Spencer was neglecting her kids, which wasn't true.

Paul Trask walked into Spencer's office and sat down on the same day the school counselor had called her, which he didn't know. But Spencer was already feeling low after the initial call. He reminded her of how much the renovation after the fire had cost them out of pocket, above what was paid by the insurance, what several leaks had cost them for their deductible, and in lost merchandise, how still not having a strong online presence was giving their competitors an advantage. Her homeless program was a noble venture that she was financing with personal money, and it had reduced the severity of the homeless population immediately around the store. But she was trying to empty the ocean with a thimble, according to Paul, and if she wanted the store to have longevity, they would have to move eventually, and they couldn't afford to do that without money from an investor.

"What are you telling me?" she asked him bluntly.

"That we need a large influx of money to remain competitive in the marketplace. It requires more than we can afford. We need one or several investors, Spencer. We have to face that. We can't hide from it anymore. And we need them soon."

"We tried. I talked to Mike Weston. He wants forty percent ownership for starters, and within two years he wants sixty to eighty percent ownership of the store. He wants to move us uptown to a store ten times this size and have branches all over the country that we'd have no control over. There is no way I'm going to let that happen. We might as well burn the place to the ground now. I'm not giving anyone sixty to eighty percent ownership of Brooke's."

"Then we need to talk to other investors. Maybe he's too big. He's used to dealing with billion-dollar companies and having control."

"He's our only option that I know of," Spencer said, looking straight at Paul. "And he's not going to bend the rules for us. He's not that kind of guy. He's nice, but business is business."

"Then negotiate with him. See if you can get him down to more reasonable percentages."

"Within two years of investing, he wants majority control. That's how they run their investments. And this won't be a big moneymaker for him. We're an oddity, kind of a little luxury snack, not a full meal. And he wants to gobble us up."

"You've got to talk to him again, Spencer. We don't have any other options right now, and I'm worried about the future. The future comes first. It's tomorrow."

"Are we in trouble now?" She looked worried too.

"No, but we will be. Sooner than you think. The world doesn't protect little specialty stores like us anymore. They'll eat us for lunch. We have to get our online shopping feature up and running in the next few months. It hurts us every day not to have it."

"I thought you hired someone to do that," she said, and frowned at him.

"I did. They're slow. I'm still waiting for their final presentation and the estimate of what it will cost us."

"Well, tell them to hurry up."

"Will you talk to Weston again?"

"We don't even know if he's still interested. I doubt he is. I was very clear with him when I rejected his offer."

"He showed up the night of the fire, that says something," Paul said, clutching at straws. He loved the store too, and wanted to protect it now and in future.

"That means he's a nice guy, it doesn't mean he wants to give us millions for the business, and not take control. Why don't you see if you can find out if he's still interested? If he is, I'll talk to him. But I guarantee you it will go nowhere. I'm not giving him sixty to eighty percent, and those are his figures."

"See if you can get him to forty and keep him there."

"He's smarter than that, Paul. And tougher. He has the money and calls the shots."

"You're smart too. He invited you to the party at the Met just so he could talk to you. That shows ingenuity and determination."

"Because he thought he could con me into giving up majority ownership. Now he knows he can't."

"I'll check around, but if he's not interested, we have to talk to others. And one day we'll have to move uptown to broaden our customer base. We have to move forward, Spencer, and move with the times."

"I'm willing. I want to, I'm even willing to consider investors, but I won't give up majority control." She was rock solid on that, and it was nonnegotiable.

"I get it," he said, standing up. "I'll let you know what I hear about Weston." She nodded, and Paul left her office, but she didn't think that anything would have changed, if Mike Weston was even interested. Mike was a smart businessman, and he wouldn't invest with them unless he could devour them, and Spencer was never going to let that happen. And Mike knew it.

Chapter 11

Paul's sources reported to him that Mike Weston would still be interested in talking. He loved the store, the quality of their merchandise, the way it was run, and the history. He'd be happy to talk to them anytime. Paul reported it to Spencer a few days after their conversation in her office.

"Give him a call. My source says he'll talk to you," Paul urged her.

"I feel like an idiot calling him," she said. "Nothing's changed, I still won't give up majority ownership. I'll be wasting his time."

"Talk to him, you never know what can happen with some artful negotiation."

"I think he has his ideas and I have mine, and we're too far apart."

"What have you got to lose?" Paul asked her.

"My credibility, and my dignity," she said humbly.

"He knows you're an honest woman. You were straight up with him before. All you can do is try again and if it's no, it's no. Maybe you can reason with him."

"Why don't you tell your source to have him call me if he's interested. That's a little less embarrassing." Paul left her office with his mission clear. He passed the message along to the person he knew in Mike's office, and two hours later, Mike called her. The response had been swift, and she was happy to hear from him.

"I hear you want to talk to me," he said, laughing. "You can call me yourself, you know, whenever you want," he reminded her. "You have an in with me."

"Thanks, Mike," she said gratefully. "How's Zack doing?"

"He's doing great. He's tired of his casts and being stuck at home a lot of the time, but he's living with me, and I love it. And he seems happy too." What Mike said confirmed what Spencer had suspected the last time they talked, that he and his wife had split up, but she still felt awkward asking him, and what he had just said sounded pretty clear. "Do you want to have a drink? We don't have to do this over the phone." And it was an excuse to see her.

"Sure. I'd love it."

"The Plaza? Five o'clock today, or six if you prefer."

"Six would be great." It meant she would miss putting the boys to bed again. It took time to get uptown, and their conversation would take a while. But this was an important meeting. She'd make it up to the boys when she got home or the next day.

"See you then," he said, and they both hung up. She was wearing a plain black summer dress and a blazer, and she wished she had worn something more exciting, but maybe it was better to be businesslike with him, for this purpose anyway.

Traffic was heavy and she was ten minutes late when she arrived. He was wearing a suit and tie, sitting at a quiet corner table, and he smiled and stood up as soon as he saw her. She tried not to be impressed by how handsome he was with his thick dark hair and strong blue eyes as she walked across the room to him. He was a striking man and everything about him exuded power in the most distinguished way. He didn't flaunt it, he wore it well. You could also tell that neither his power nor his success was new. They were part of his persona and his charm.

She sat down at the table with him, and he ordered a glass of wine for each of them.

"I was happy to hear that the deal wasn't completely dead in your mind. The last time we talked, I didn't think I'd be hearing from you on that subject again. You sounded very definite." He looked at her warmly.

"I was. I am," she said honestly. "But we need an investor. Paul says we can't stay abreast of the times without one, and he's probably right. And if we have to have an investor, I'd rather it be you than anyone else. If we can come to decent terms for both of us." That was the key issue here. And the last time they spoke of it, they were as far apart as anyone could get. "We're working on the online shopping feature. Paul thinks we have to move uptown eventually. The neighborhood scares some people, although it's not dangerous. I'm not ready to move yet."

"He's right. Being where you are is hurting your sales."

"The homeless people wandering around are harmless. They don't look great, but they've never hurt anyone."

"There's talk of drug gangs on the borders there, and that **is** dangerous." She nodded. If it was true, he was right. "How are your kids?" he asked, breaking away from business for a minute, and happy to see her.

"They're fine," she said, sighing, "except I got a call from their school a few days ago. Apparently, the school counselor thinks I'm never home, and I don't spend enough time with the boys. They're not complaining and I'm with them on the weekends, well, after work on Saturday until Sunday night. In retail, you have to work on Saturdays."

"That's familiar turf for me. Zack and I are catching up now, and we're getting to know each other. I missed a lot of time with my kids, and it's hard to catch up later, but I get the feeling you do spend time with yours," he said generously.

"I try to. What do other women do who work? It's a juggling act at best."

"My wife was lucky. She didn't work, but she wasn't with them all the time either. No one is, unless you can't afford a babysitter, then you have no choice. They don't see their father?" She shook her head.

"Very seldom. We got divorced when they were toddlers, and fatherhood isn't his strong suit. He sees them every once in a while and brings them back two hours later. They're a handful. He'll probably get married again and have another family and be ready for it. But he's missed the boat on the twins so far." Mike realized again that she had a lot to cope with, especially compared to someone like Maureen, who had nothing to do except play tennis and complain. Spencer was a much more exciting woman, and he was sure that what she did wasn't easy. And she was busy with her work and all the problems and demands, not just her kids.

"I'm getting divorced," he said out of the blue, bringing her up on his own news.

"I sort of suspected that when you said Zack was living with you. Is it going okay?"

"More or less. Our marriage has been dead for years. We never had the guts to bury it. I finally did. I couldn't take the punishment anymore for everything I didn't do and hadn't done all the times I worked late or traveled. She's been wearing her anger and bitterness like a shroud for years. It was killing both of us. All of a sudden, I couldn't see the point of being punished for the rest of my life. The practical stuff is a little complicated, but she's fairly reasonable. I feel like I just got out of prison. I'm sorry to say that. It sounds disrespectful and ungrateful, but it's true." She smiled as he said it. He looked so earnest. "I should have done it years ago. She was never going to forgive me, so what's the point?" He looked peaceful as he said it.

"Did the kids take it okay?"

"I flew out to see my daughter in San Francisco to tell her, and she was fine with me. She wasn't surprised. I think she was relieved too. The atmosphere has been poisonous for years, and she and her mother don't get along. Jennifer is too much like me, which irritates her mother. Zack was sad about it when I told him on the plane flying back from France. We were waiting till he got home to tell him. He's adjusting pretty well. He says he wants to live with me, but that could change. And he's finally going to college at the end of the year. Right now, he's spending days at his mother's and nights with me, because he can't manage with his casts. So, I guess it's all turning out okay." He smiled at her. He didn't look unhappy. In fact, he looked more relaxed than when she'd last seen him. And at the Met, the icy tension between him and his wife had been palpable.

"I think I'll be poorer, but a lot happier. I'm not going to sacrifice my life to save on a divorce. If I live another forty or fifty years, I don't want to be unhappy for all that. That's what finally convinced me. Life is short, but it can be long too. Too long to be miserable." He smiled at Spencer, and then they got back to business. "So, what are we going to do about your store? I take it you've given it some more thought, or we wouldn't be here."

"I have, and I always come out in the same place. It hurts, but I could live with the thirty-five or forty percent investment you spoke about initially. But the jump after that to your owning sixty to eighty percent of the business would kill me. I can't give that up, Mike. I've worked too hard to preserve

Brooke's and bring it this far to give up control to someone else."

"The trouble is," he said quietly, "no one will invest in it unless you do. Those are the kind of percentages people expect, and I do too. And there's no way to turn Brooke's into a big moneymaker unless you make the kind of changes I was suggesting, make it exponentially bigger, move it uptown, or downtown, open branches around the country. It's the kind of growth my investors would expect." He was matter-of-fact about it, although sympathetic to how she felt.

"It wouldn't be the same store then," she said sadly.

"No, it wouldn't," he admitted.

"You wouldn't accept less ownership?"

"I couldn't. And you won't make enough increase in profits unless someone puts a lot of money into it. Or you can keep it a small specialty store, but then it's not an interesting investment for someone like me. You've got to go big and spend big to earn big, and it's tough to do with the model of a store like Brooke's, if you hang onto majority control and don't give the investors a free hand to do what they need to do." He looked regretful as he said it, and so did she. He knew how much the store meant to her, and how hard it was for her to let go.

"I can't give up majority control, Mike. Not to that degree."

"I know," he said kindly, "but that's what any big investor will want."

"We don't need stores all over the country, or a huge store. You can't maintain the quality control that way." He knew that too.

"At a certain point, it's about revenue and return on the investment more than quality. There's going to be some slippage if you grow." She nodded. He was being honest with her.

"It's everything my grandfather didn't want, and I've been committed to maintain."

"If you want serious investment money, you'll have to give up control." It sounded like a death sentence to her.

"I'm not that desperate yet. We're doing okay."

"Okay isn't good enough. Paul Trask is right. You won't last long with 'okay.' Only the big fish survive now, the small ones don't. In order for my investors to accept a deal like yours, we'd have to own a very heavy majority. I can't negotiate that down. No one would want the deal. Why don't you think about it? The kind of money you could make on it long-term would be an important legacy for your boys. The money matters too."

"I'd be giving up and betraying everything I've

stood for. I'd be the sellout, the traitor. I can't do that." She looked him squarely in the eye and he respected her for everything she stood for but they both knew there was no way to make a deal.

"You're a woman of principle, Spencer. But you're paying a high price for those principles."

"Better that than selling my soul, and my grand-father's legacy."

They had another glass of wine and talked about other things, but the deal they'd been talking about weighed heavily on them both. It was never going to happen. He wanted to invest in the store, but he had to do it on his terms, he couldn't on hers.

"What about a smaller investor, who would ask for less?" she asked him.

"You won't get enough return on the deal for a small investment. And a big investor wants control. That's how those deals work." She knew it too.

She was quiet when they walked out to the street. It had been a futile effort meeting him to negotiate, and he looked unhappy. He would have loved to invest in Brooke's and work with her, but not on her terms.

"Call me if I can do anything," he said as they stood on the sidewalk. He didn't want to insult her by saying "if you change your mind," because he knew she wouldn't. She was too proud to give up her principles and too honorable to let her grand-father down, even if it meant giving up millions from an investor who would take control and change the store forever.

They lingered for a few minutes, neither of them wanting to leave.

"I'm sorry I wasted your time, Mike," she said sincerely.

"You didn't. I loved seeing you. I wish I could find a way to make it work, in a better way for you."

"Yeah, me too. We'll be fine as we are," she said bravely, and he knew they would be for a while, and then one day they wouldn't, with the model they had now. What he was offering her was a se-cure future, but the end of a dream. Spencer still believed in dreams.

He shared a cab with her to go downtown, and dropped her off at her house in Chelsea. She didn't invite him in for another drink. It was late by then, and they were both tired, and she wanted to see her boys. It had been a disappointing meeting. Paul was foolish to have her try to negotiate with Mike again. There was no negotiation possible. It was either give up control or there was no deal. She watched Mike in the cab as it drove away, and wondered if she'd ever see him again.

* * *

233

Mike was eating pizza and watching TV with Zack when Jenny called them that night. She talked to her brother, and then her father.

"Did you see the article in **The New York Times** on Sunday about Spencer Brooke?" she asked him.

"No." And Spencer hadn't mentioned it when they had drinks. Maybe she had forgotten. "I just had a meeting with her. What did it say?"

"She started something called 'Free Love' in an old garage downtown in a bad neighborhood. They're giving away bags of brand-new clothes and tools and food and supplies to homeless people. There are signs on the windows of the store about it. In exchange, they've made a discreet request that the homeless people not camp out in front of the store, because it upsets their customers. And so far, it's working. But Spencer Brooke is giving away a fortune in new goods to the homeless people who turn up to get them. A hundred bags a week so far, and they're thinking of giving more. They hand it out one or two nights a week, with a small staff to pack the bags they give away and hand them out. She's paying for it all herself, it's not paid for by the store." Mike was silent for a moment, thinking about it. She hadn't said a word about her project. It was a stroke of brilliance to use it as gentle persuasion to get the homeless to stop camping out in front of the store. She was helping them and the store at the same time.

"She's an amazing woman," he said to Jenny. "I just turned down her deal again, or more precisely, she turned down mine. She won't give up control of the store, and she'd have to for us to want to invest in it."

"She must love the store a lot," Jenny said quietly.

"She does," he said.

"It shows. I'd really love to meet her sometime, Dad. I'd love to work for her. Maybe I can next summer, and then I'd be in New York, and I could stay with you too."

"You can stay with me anytime, and I'd be happy to introduce you to Spencer whenever you want. I wonder why she didn't tell me about her project," except he knew why. She was a profoundly modest woman, and didn't want to brag about what she was doing. The project sounded remarkable to him. And if Jenny hadn't mentioned it, he'd never have known. He had been so busy lately with Zack, he had just scanned the papers on some days.

"You should donate to Free Love, Dad," Jenny suggested, sounding passionate about it.

"She didn't ask me to or tell me about it. I'll have to look into it. Thanks for telling me about the article." He looked it up after they ended the call, and it was all there. There were no photographs, in order to respect people's privacy, but he was vastly impressed by the description of the project, and Spencer for organizing it.

He was sorry that he couldn't give her the investment money she needed to give longevity to the store. But if she wouldn't give up majority control, there was nothing he could do, and he understood her reasons for it.

He read the article again that night after Zack went to bed and he was alone. She was a remarkable woman, and he wished there was more that he could do for her. Instead, she did for everyone else, even for her grandfather long after he was gone, at her own expense. And Mike couldn't do anything to help. She was on her own.

Chapter 12

Mike was watching TV with Zack, as they did every night. It was a British spy series that they'd been following together since Zack got back, and Mike switched to the late-night news when the episode was over. Zack rolled himself to his bedroom in the chair. He was getting quite adept at fending for himself, and couldn't wait to get his casts off. They had settled into a friendly routine together.

Mike was watching the local news when a familiar sight filled the screen. It was Brooke's, lit up with police in riot gear filling the street around it. The announcer explained that a full-blown war had erupted downtown, between two rival gangs of drug dealers on the edge of Chelsea. Some big shipment of drugs had been delivered from South America, and there was a shootout between rival distributors in the two gangs. Three men had been shot on one side, and two on the other, a passerby had been injured, and one police officer was in critical condition. The narcotics squad was there in full force, and SWAT teams, and shots rang out while the announcer explained the situation from a covered position at a safe distance. And behind the scene of carnage sat Spencer's store.

She saw it on TV at the same time Mike did, and heard the announcer say that there was some concern that looting might occur. Two of the store's windows had been shattered and the glass had been completely shot out of one of them, giving easy access to the store known for its expensive, exclusive merchandise. Burglar alarms could be heard sounding in the distance as Spencer hurriedly put on shoes and a denim jacket with her jeans and T-shirt and rushed to tell Francine she was going out. She didn't say where or why.

She found a cab in a few minutes to travel the short distance to the store. There were police officers and barricades blocking traffic, and they stopped the cab a few blocks from the store. Spencer paid the driver and got out and spoke to one of the officers. There were ambulances speeding by.

"You can't go down that street, miss." A police

officer wearing a bulletproof vest stopped her. "Do you live there?"

Spencer pointed to the lit-up hulk of Brooke's. "That's my store."

"There's active gunfire." They heard shots ring out in the distance after he said it, and Spencer looked at him, shocked.

"Are they looting the store?" she asked.

"Not yet," he said, and listened to something on the radio. Another officer was down, and one of the shooters had been killed by the rival gang. It was a mad scene of heavily armed police officers, riot troops, SWAT teams, and emergency vehicles. As the officer turned to say something to a colleague, Spencer slipped quietly down the street, staying close to the buildings. She just wanted to see what was happening at the store, and if anyone was climbing through the shattered windows, or stealing what was in them. But there was no sign of entering near the windows, as she huddled in a doorway, watching the action. The gunfire had slowed down to an occasional shot, and the entire area had been sealed off to keep people out. There was no one on the street except police, and presumably gang members hiding in doorways and behind cars, taking aim at each other and the police.

Spencer had been there for half an hour without moving when a cluster of armed men in motley clothes carrying a variety of weapons ran toward the store and started to climb through the windows. She didn't know if their intention was to loot the store or to take refuge from the police shooting at them. Several men ran through the open windows and disappeared into the store as Spencer moved closer to the scene, although she knew there was nothing she could do to stop them, if the police couldn't do it with gunfire. All she could think of was the damage they would do, so soon after the fire. It silenced forever the argument that the neighborhood was safe. There was no way she could claim that now, with rival gangs in the drug trade shooting at each other, and police crouching behind cars, taking cover, and shooting at them. Helicopters were hovering overhead. She couldn't believe what she was seeing and that the store was being invaded by gangs. She could only imagine the kind of damage they were going to do by the time it was over. There were tears rolling down her cheeks and she didn't even know she was crying.

Her cell phone rang while she watched, just far enough away to be out of danger. All the action was closer to the store.

It was Beau. "Are you watching this horror on TV?" he asked her.

"No . . . yes . . ." She didn't want him to know that she was there. She was too frightened to move now. More men ran into the store. The police shot one of them and he lay sprawled in one of the windows, writhing in pain, until two more officers dragged him out of the window and paramedics took him away.

"Oh my God, this is crazy," Beau said, terrified by what he was seeing on the screen.

"I'll call you back," she said to Beau, and hung up. She didn't want to talk to anyone. Marcy called her too and she didn't answer. The store was now the scene of an ongoing shootout, as several more of the gang members ran through the windows into the store and began shooting each other as the two gangs collided again. And the store was an ideal place for the bad guys and the police to play hide-and-seek.

Mike was watching it, mesmerized at home. He picked up his cell phone and called Spencer's number. She didn't want to talk to him either but answered anyway. She could hardly think, she was so shocked by what was happening.

"Are you watching this?" She heard Mike's voice and nodded, struggling to find her voice. She was terrified by what she was seeing and hearing.

"Yes, I am," she said softly, never taking her eyes off the men rushing in and out of the store windows. And she saw two of them shatter two more windows, for easy entry. The others had been shot out by gunfire earlier. And then Mike realized something. The sounds he heard coming through her cell phone were different from the more muted ones he heard on TV, where the prevailing sound in the background was sirens. On Spencer's phone he kept hearing the staccato of gunshots that didn't sound distant at all.

"Where are you?" he asked her.

"Here. I'm watching the store. The bad guys keep running through the windows into the store, and now they're shooting each other, and the police are shooting them."

"Oh my God, you're down there?" Somehow, he had known she would be, which was why he had called her, to make sure she was okay. "Where are you?" he asked again.

"A little less than half a block from the store. I'm in a doorway. No one can see me, I'm okay."

"Spencer, get out of there, go home. There's nothing you can do. They won't let you go inside anyway, even when the shooting's over. It's a crime scene."

"It's my store. I want to go in when the shooting stops."

"They won't let you. Get out of there." All it would take was one stray bullet to kill her. "Go back down the street you came. I'll pick you up in a cab." His voice was strong and firm.

"I'm not leaving," she said stubbornly.

Mike was shouting at her then, and Zack came back from his bedroom in his wheelchair to see what was happening.

"Spencer, get out of there! Can you get into the building you're in front of?" She tried the door handle.

"No, it's locked. I'm safe where I am. I'll call you later," she said, and hung up and continued watching the carnage happening in front of her. Twenty minutes later, the gunfire had stopped, and a full SWAT team entered the building. There was no further gunfire, and minutes later they radioed other police and SWAT teams to enter. Only one man was led out alive, covered in blood. The others inside were all dead. They had shot each other. It was said to be the bloodiest gang war in New York in years, over a recent delivery of heroin that had come in by ship from South America.

As the police came out of the store again, through the windows, and the bodies were brought out on gurneys through the front door, with the alarms still sounding, Spencer came out of the doorway where she had been concealed for nearly an hour and approached the shattered windows of the store. Two police officers barred her way immediately, as she looked up at them with a determined expression.

"Get behind the barrier," one of them shouted at her. They still weren't a hundred percent certain that there weren't additional shooters hiding somewhere inside.

"This is my store," she said, and didn't move an inch. "I want to go in and see how bad the damage is."

"We're still bringing the bodies out," one of the officers told her, and she stood her ground next to him.

"Then I'll wait." The two officers looked at her, and one of them asked for her ID. She handed it to them, and her business card, and they nodded.

"You still have to wait. You can't go in yet." She nodded and took a step back so she wouldn't get in their way, but didn't leave.

Half an hour later all the bodies were out. There was blood on what was left of the displays in the windows, including a beige alpaca and sable blanket draped over an antique Louis XV chair. The blanket was priced at $100,000 and was splattered with blood. All the window displays had been destroyed, all the mannequins knocked down. Spencer cautiously approached the building, and while a cluster of NYPD police were talking to each other, she hopped up to one of the windows and walked inside. No one saw her go in. She bumped her arm against a shard of glass hanging from one of the window frames and paid no attention to it as she slipped inside. There was blood everywhere on the floors. Displays had been knocked over, vitrines had been shattered by gunfire, a wall of perfumes had been shot out and the perfumes were running down the wall. On the floor there was a bloodstained running shoe that had come off one of the bodies when they removed it. Police photographers were taking pictures of the scene and one of them looked up and saw her. They looked shocked to see each other.

"What are you doing here?" he called out to her, thinking she was there to steal something.

"I own the store." She pulled her ID out of her pocket and handed it to him.

"You shouldn't be here. Something could fall, and you'll get hurt."

"I wanted to see how bad the damage was. Did they go upstairs?"

"We don't know yet." He turned to his partner then. "Take her outside." The police officer led Spencer back through the windows, and she saw that the sleeve of her jacket was drenched in blood, and it was running down her arm. The officer helped her down out of the window and signaled to a paramedic. "She's hurt," he shouted, and the paramedic came running with a gurney for her.

"I'm fine," she insisted, as he looked her over quickly and pointed to her arm.

"Were you shot?" She shook her head. He pulled back her sleeve and exposed the nasty gash she'd gotten from the shard of glass in the window. The cut was so fine she hadn't felt it. It had cut her like a scalpel, and blood was gushing from the wound as a tall man came forward and spoke to the paramedic.

"That needs to be sewn up." Spencer looked up and saw that it was Mike.

"What are you doing here?" she asked him, shocked.

"I came to get you. I'm taking you to the hospital." The paramedic pulled a bandage out of a kit and offered to send her in an ambulance. She tried to tell them she was fine, but Mike and the paramedic lifted her into it, and Mike climbed in with her. "Why is it that I know now that wherever there's trouble, I'm going to find you in the thick of it?" He held her other hand as they careened through the night with the siren screaming. "How bad did the store look?" he asked her softly. He could tell she'd gone inside, which was how she'd cut her arm.

"Pretty bad. A lot of blood. A lot of them got killed in there, except one guy, and he was shot too."

They got to NYU Medical Center quickly. Mike climbed out of the ambulance behind Spencer and followed her inside, while one of the paramedics pushed her in a wheelchair. The bandage on her arm was a dark burgundy color by then. She was losing blood at a rapid rate and Mike was worried. It had been foolish of her to push into the store, but it was too late to say it now.

He waited in the emergency room with her while they cleaned the wound and tried to stop the bleeding, and she looked faint for a minute as he gently held her shoulders. The doctor came in quickly, gave her a tetanus shot and a shot to anesthetize the arm, and sewed it up carefully. She was in shock from all she'd seen, and from her injury, and her teeth were chattering while the doctor sewed her up. The nurses had cut off her denim jacket and her T-shirt, and covered her with a hospital gown, as Mike stayed with her and never left her side.

The police took a statement from her to make sure she wasn't one of the active victims of the gangs, and she inquired what would happen at the store. They said that the police would be there all night, protecting the crime scene and taking evidence, so she knew the store was safe until morning. She had a long bandage on her arm, and she looked pale and felt dizzy when she and Mike left the hospital together. Mike hailed a cab, and covered her with his own jacket over the hospital gown she was wearing with her jeans. He had been sure she would try to enter the store as soon as she could, and he was right.

"I'm taking you home." He gave the driver her address, and put an arm around her as they walked inside. He was afraid that she might faint, but she was steadier once she got a breath of the cool air. She had her house key and the keys to the store in her pocket.

"Do you want to come in?" she asked him, and he nodded. He was impressed by everything he'd seen that night, and by how bold Spencer had been going into the store to check it out. She was fearless when it came to protecting what she loved.

He followed her into the front hall of her orderly house, and she walked him into the kitchen. Ben and Axel's toys were there, and there was a pretty garden outside with a set of swings.

"Do you want something to eat?" she asked him.

"Let's get you to bed. You've had a rough night." He had a strong protective presence.

"I'm okay," she said, and sat in a chair at the table. "Can I have some ice cream?" she asked him, and he smiled. She looked like a beautiful child with her long blond hair hanging down her back. She pointed to where the bowls were, and he scooped some ice cream out for both of them and sat down next to her.

"That was insane tonight, Spencer. You were

crazy to go inside. One of the shooters might still have been alive." He shuddered at the thought.

"The cops had already gone in and the gunfire had stopped. They didn't let me stay. The main floor is a mess."

"You can get it cleaned up. Don't think about it now."

"I guess you're right about the neighborhood," she said sadly. "Our customers will be terrified to go there now."

"We can talk about it tomorrow, but Spencer, you need partners. You can't do it alone." He was thinking that maybe she should sell the store. It was too much for any one person. "I want us to figure out a deal where we can invest and I can help you. Between fires and drug dealers and looters and God knows what, and the homeless, you're a one-woman army. I'm worried about you."

"I'm okay. I can handle it," she said, with a chocolate ice cream mustache on her lip, and he smiled.

"You're a holy terror."

"I'm keeping the store for the boys one day." He had guessed that. They were the next generation, but they were years away from being able to take over. She'd be ready to retire by then, if ever.

"What if they don't want it?" he asked her seriously. "Kids are unpredictable."

"Then they'll sell it, but I won't. That'll be up to them."

"Would you let them?"

"Maybe. It'll be their decision then. I'm the gatekeeper for now."

"That's a hard job," he said, just thinking about that night. "You have to move the store now."

"I'll start looking. Maybe something temporary, until we sell the building." She hiccupped on a sob as she realized what she had just said and what it meant.

As soon as she finished her ice cream, he put their bowls in the sink and looked at her. "I'm putting you to bed. Where's your bedroom?"

"Upstairs." She walked upstairs with Mike behind her. She was at the opposite end of the hall from Francine and the boys, with a door that closed off her suite. He followed her in, closed the door, and waited in her bedroom while she took off her jacket and the blood-splattered hospital gown and put on a cozy cashmere nightgown. It wasn't a seduction scene, he wanted to make sure she didn't faint or fall or hit her head or go into shock again. She came out of the bathroom in her pink cashmere nightgown and a flowered D. Porthault robe.

"Now get into bed," he said, and she giggled. The bandage on her arm looked enormous on her thin arm, and there was still blood seeping through, and it was starting to hurt. The anesthetic had worn off. She slid into her bed between the sheets, and he sat down on the bed next to her and stroked her hair, and then he bent down and kissed her gently on the lips. She was startled but it felt natural and right to her. The effect on him was searing, but he had no intention of following through now. The night had been too traumatic, for her, worrying about the store, and for him, terrified she would be killed once he knew where she was. "That's all you get tonight," he said with a smile, as she smiled up at him. "You're an amazing woman. But you can't do it all yourself. We'll talk about everything to-morrow." He kissed her again, and then he went to sit in a chair, before he could do something he might regret later, and stretched his legs out ahead of him to watch her sleep. He didn't want to leave her and she didn't mind his being there. She liked it. She opened her eyes once or twice to make sure he was still there. He didn't say anything, he just watched her as she drifted back to sleep and he sat in the chair to be sure she was all right, and eventually he dozed off too, exhausted after the traumatic evening, and worried about her.

Mike woke up with a start with the sun streaming into the room, and a little blond boy in pajamas staring at him. Mike smiled at him, and whispered to him so they didn't wake Spencer, who was sleeping soundly.

"Hi, I'm Mike. I'm a friend of your mom's."

"I'm Axel. Do you like pancakes?" Mike followed him out of the room, so they didn't disturb his mother, and Axel's identical twin was waiting for him on the stairs. Mike went down to the kitchen with them, where Francine was making pancakes and looked at Mike in surprise. She didn't question who he was but could guess his presence was related to the shooting. She had assumed that Spencer had gone to meet with police once she knew she was out.

"Did everything turn out okay last night?" she asked Mike. She had seen the news on the TV in her room but it wasn't over yet when she turned it off.

"Relatively. It was quite a scene." He didn't want to go into detail in front of the boys. "I'm Mike, by the way." The boys chattered all through breakfast, and showed him their car collection, and he tried hard but couldn't tell them apart. He wrote Spencer a note, peeked into her room, saw that she was still asleep, and left it next to her bed. He said goodbye to Francine and the boys and took a cab back to his apartment. It was still early, and Zack was still asleep. Mike showered and dressed and left for the office. He knew Zack could get up by himself now. He kept thinking about Spencer, braving the scene last night. He didn't know how he would do it, but he had to find a deal that worked for her, at least to help her move the store to a safer location. He couldn't let go of wanting to protect her. He had no idea how he'd do it, but he had to. And as he took a cab to his office, the one thing he knew was that when he kissed her the night before, he meant it. He wanted to do that since the first trip he'd met her. And he'd been so relieved that she had survived the night before that he didn't hold back anymore.

Chapter 13

The aftermath of the drug war on the Brooke's doorstep was much more complicated to deal with than the results of the fire. When Spencer woke up, the boys had already left for school. She read the note Mike had left on her night table. All it said was "Please take it easy today. Love, Mike." She called Marcy as soon as she was awake enough to ask what was happening.

"We closed the store. We got a company in that specializes in cleaning up crime scenes. Five men died on the main floor last night, and one made it up the stairs and died in Men's Shoes. The carpet there is shot."

"I was there right after they took out the bodies," Spencer said calmly.

"How did you get in?"

"Through the windows. I went down there while they were still shooting. I went in right after, but the police wouldn't let me stay." She didn't tell Marcy she'd been injured. "I'm sorry I overslept today. What are you doing about the windows?"

"Having them replaced. It'll take a week, so they're boarding them up now. Paul wants a meeting," she said ominously. "Are you coming in?"

"I'll be there in half an hour," Spencer promised. She was surprised to find that her legs were shaky as she took a shower and dressed, and she felt weak. The night had taken more of a toll than she expected. And her arm was throbbing. She'd had to keep it out of the shower because of the stitches. She texted Mike on her way to work and thanked him for staying with her the night before.

When she got to the store, it was eerily quiet. The special cleaning crew was hard at work, cleaning up the bloodstains, another crew was cleaning up the broken glass, and store employees were collecting the ruined merchandise. Paul and Marcy were waiting for her in Paul's office. Paul looked acutely worried.

"We have some decisions to make," he said, as soon as she sat down. She had worn a long-sleeve sweater, so they didn't see her bandage. She had had to throw the denim jacket away at the hospital.

The nurses had cut it to shreds, and it was stained with blood. "It's not a conversation anymore. We have to give up this location. It's done. I know you love it, Spencer, but it's not safe anymore. No one will come here after last night." She didn't argue with him. She knew he was right. "For now, we need to find a temporary location. Marcy has been researching it this morning. It's going to be costly, but we don't have a choice. Even though Brooke's had nothing to do with the shooting, we'll be associated with it, and men died in the building. That's the kiss of death to any store, especially one like ours." Spencer nodded again.

"I know none of us want to, but I think we need to sell the building. We can stay in a temporary location until then, use the money from the sale, and borrow the rest to buy a new building. I think it's the only way we can manage it. With luck, we'll find something with personality and charm. But I think even your grandfather would have agreed, this location is finished for us. Competing in retail is hard enough today, staying in a dangerous place is suicide. If the gangs are moving in here, and apparently they are, we're done." Paul looked somber as he said it.

"I think the plan makes sense," Spencer said quietly. Both of them were surprised that she put up no resistance. She knew when they'd been beaten by events. "How fast do you think we'll find a temporary location?"

"I don't know. Marcy and I called every commercial realtor in the city this morning. There's one possibility in Soho on lower Broadway. There's nothing uptown right now. And downtown is more expensive, it's in higher demand. Given who our customers are, we'll be better off uptown. They've been coming downtown for years. Maybe it's time we make things easier for them, and it will bring a flock of new customers."

"How much do you think we'll have to borrow?" she asked Paul.

"It depends on what we find. But it'll cost us a lot."

"Can we afford it?"

"We'll have to. If we open our online shopping soon, and broaden our client base with a new location, then we can. In a way, this location has been holding us back."

"We have an appointment to see the location on Broadway this afternoon," Marcy told her. "I'll go with you."

When they went to see it, it was brutally ugly, in need of repairs, poorly located, too small, and shockingly expensive.

Mike called her when she got back to the office. Sounding discouraged, she told him about the temporary store they'd just seen and how bad it was, and how expensive.

"I called some people too," Mike said. "It seems as though there's nothing available right now. I only inquired about uptown."

"We asked about both. Paul wants to put our building on the market. I hate to sell it. And it will be harder to sell now, except for some other purpose. He doesn't think we have a choice."

"You don't." Mike sounded sympathetic.

"I want to go over the numbers of your offer with you again," she said somberly. She sounded as though she was walking to the guillotine, and he felt terrible about it.

"Don't do that if you don't want to."

"I don't, but I have no choice, do I? We're going to have to buy an expensive building, and probably won't get a lot for ours. Having a bunch of drug dealers shoot each other right in our store doesn't exactly increase the value of the real estate. We have to be realistic if we want Brooke's to survive," she said. He could hear the sadness in her voice.

"Why don't you take a few days and let the dust settle before we talk numbers again," he said. "Keep looking at temporary locations. And I'll see what turns up at my end. I'll ask my father. Sometimes he knows about some interesting deals. Between the two of us we know all the big commercial real estate brokers. Something will turn up. Are you going to reopen downtown in the meantime?"

"I don't know," Spencer said, feeling lost. "They're scraping the blood off the walls now."

"How's your arm?" he asked. He worried about her. Her life was so hard sometimes, with so much on her shoulders. It didn't seem fair. She faced it so bravely and honorably. And he had a feeling she was about to do something she'd regret. He could tell that she was seriously considering the deal he had offered her, and he felt guilty about it now. She would lose all control of her store if she did that. But she had her back to the wall, with no better offers or options.

Zack asked him about it that night when they ate dinner together.

"What happened with that story about the drug war last night? You were very interested in it."

"Two gangs of drug dealers got in a shooting war over a big shipment of heroin that came in. It all happened in front of that store I was thinking of investing in, the one that your sister likes so much. In fact, they broke into the store before it was all over, and five of them died there, and one of the cops."

"Sounds ugly," Zack said. "What happens in a

case like that? Do they close the store? Would any-one still shop there?"

"Probably not. They won't close but they have to move, which is an expensive proposition. They're not too happy about it."

"Yeah, I bet they're not. Is there blood all over the place?" Mike nodded. "Are you still going to invest in it, or is it a bad investment now?" Zack was more interested in his father's business than he had been before his year in Europe.

"I don't know. I might. The owner turned my original offer down."

"Why?" Zack looked puzzled.

"Because the terms of the deal were tough. They'd have to give up the controlling interest in the store, and the investors and I would control it."

"That doesn't sound very fair." Zack looked surprised.

"It's not, but that's the way business is some-times. When people want something or need money badly, they pay a high price for it."

"And you take advantage of it," Zack said, and his father didn't answer for a minute.

"I guess we do."

"That's why I don't like business. It's not nice." Zack put it so simply, but it was true. "Do you think they'll take your deal now?" Zack asked him.

"They might have to. I think they're considering it. It's a big decision for them."

"Sucks for them. First a bunch of drug dealers kill each other in their store, and then they lose control of their business. They must be pretty miserable." Mike realized that Zack had summed it up perfectly. And that some of Spencer's misery was due to him.

Jenny called that night too. She had read about the downtown shootout in the online news at school, and she had seen that Brooke's was involved and some of the drug dealers had shot each other there, after breaking into the store during the shootout.

"How awful. Did they mess up the store?"

"Some."

"Will they fix it? It's such a beautiful store. It's like a little jewel."

"They're going to move. The neighborhood just isn't safe anymore."

"Will the owner continue her homeless program?" Jenny was concerned for Spencer, even though she didn't know her.

"She says they will, wherever they move to. They're looking for a temporary location now. They haven't found anything yet."

"How sad. How terrible that people broke into the store to shoot each other."

"It was pretty bad." He didn't tell her that he'd been there or that the owner had gotten hurt. Jenny gave him her news but had really only called to comment on the shooting at Brooke's, which shocked her when she read about it. Mike's children were both very compassionate about it, which touched him.

Spencer called him two days later. Mike had been giving her some space to recover. She had seen two more temporary locations by then, smaller, uglier, and even more expensive than the first one. The store was still closed, and they hadn't made a decision yet about whether to reopen, or when, before a move.

"I'd like to talk to you when you have time," she said. He could guess what it was about, and Zack's comments leapt to mind.

"Do you want to come to my office, or should I come to your place?" he asked her. She was working from home since the store was closed. And Marcy, Beau, and Paul were working from home too. There was a skeleton staff at the store in their offices to tend to things like accounting, and to keep current with their bills.

"What's best for you?" she asked him.

"Why don't I come by at the end of the day today, on my way home? Does that work for you?"

"That's fine." She was painfully quiet, which disturbed him. She was normally so full of energy, and now she sounded so subdued.

She was waiting for him in slacks and a sweater when he arrived. He could hear her children squealing and laughing upstairs. It sounded like bath time, and they were having fun. Spencer offered him wine and he declined. He decided that he'd better be cold sober for this meeting. He didn't want to do or say the wrong thing. She looked worn out and very pale.

"I've been looking over the offer you made me," she said quietly, "the one I turned down before. Things have changed in a short time. Paul says we have to sell the building, so we can eventually afford to buy a new one. And it's going to take a lot more money than we'll get for our current location. We won't get much for it in that neighborhood now, especially after the other night. The location we have now is going to be a real bargain for someone. But it makes no sense to keep it, and we can't afford to. We'll need all the money we can get to buy a new building, or even lease one long-term. And we'd need your help with that." He nodded. That would have been part of the deal if she had accepted.

"What stuck in my throat before and I just couldn't live with is that I'd give up majority ownership of the store, and lose all control to you and your investors. I felt as if I was betraying my grandfather. But realistically, I just have no choice." She was a practical person, despite her loyalty to her grandfather's principles. And she wanted the store to survive.

"You wanted forty percent ownership the first year, which was fine with me and seemed reasonable if you're going to invest to the degree you said you would. And a new building will cost us both a fortune, in the right location, particularly uptown, which is where most of our clients live, so that makes the most sense.

"You wanted another twenty percent ownership from me in the second year, which would put you up to sixty percent ownership within a year. So, within a year you'd be the majority owner, and have control of the business. And a year after that, another twenty, which would bring you to eighty percent ownership. And I'd have a very small voice in the business, and no control whatsoever, with you as eighty percent owners, and me only having twenty percent."

He felt guilty listening to her, particularly at the look in her eyes. She looked devastated, but was being painfully gracious about it, and polite.

She didn't blame him for the situation they were in, or anyone but herself. And it wasn't her fault either. It was a result of the times they lived in, and of the Brookes having established themselves in a dubious neighborhood to begin with, that had gotten worse.

"I could soften the third installment," Mike said in a low voice, "and make it only fifteen, which would give us seventy-five percent ownership in the end, rather than eighty. I think our investors would be satisfied with that. It's a very strong position for us, as investors."

"And a terrible one for me," she admitted, but with no other options and no choice. The shootout had pushed their situation over the edge.

"Well, you've summed it up very succinctly," Mike said. "And I fully understand why you don't want it." He wasn't sure why she'd invited him to go over it again. They both understood his offer and their respective positions.

"I actually invited you here to tell you that I accept. I really don't have a choice. We need an influx of money to keep the name and the store alive. It won't be the same store under different ownership, but I hope you'll do your best to respect what it was," she said with quiet dignity, to such a degree that it tore at his heart. She looked so brave and strong as she sat there watching him. He wanted to put his arms around her, but not while they were talking business.

"Don't forget that part of that deal was a long-term management contract for you to continue running the business as you have until now, so that it does, in fact, remain the same store. We offered you a ten-year contract," he said, "at a high salary, to protect the brand."

"I couldn't do that," she said quietly. "I'd be willing to stay for the first year, while I still have majority ownership, but once that changes after a year, I wouldn't want to stay. It would be too painful to watch everything change." So, she was willing to break her heart and give him her grandfather's business on a silver platter, but she was not willing to sell herself as a slave, at any price. "I wouldn't be willing to stay longer than that first year," she said firmly, "but you'd have the store, and all the information I could provide before I leave. I could use that year to make sure that the transition goes smoothly," she said with a sad smile.

"You're the life and soul of that store," he said passionately. "Without you, it would be meaningless, just a store like any other, with a lot of expensive merchandise. You're what makes it all work, Spencer."

"You'd have all my notes and our records to follow. You could easily do it without me. You'd have the template for it. You won't need me at all." But he did, in more ways than she realized, and just as much for the store. She was a beguiling creature with a magic touch, like the homeless program she had organized that was working so well. It was a gift from the heart. What she was offering would have no life and no soul without her, but he also understood from what she was saying that she couldn't be bought. Basically, she was handing over her business to him, and her grandfather's dream, and planning to jump ship in a year, once she no longer had control. After that, she had no interest in staying. In a way, he didn't blame her, but the deal was much less appealing without her, if at all.

"I'll have to think about it," he said when he stood up. "I'll let you know." He was shocked that she had accepted his terms and was willing to give him majority control, on his terms, but she was no longer part of the deal, which took all the magic out of it for him. He was excited to work with her, but not just to oversee a high-end store. And he knew perfectly well that without her, the soul of Brooke's would be gone. She was the ephemeral secret ingredient that made it all work.

It had been a huge step to be willing to give him eighty percent of the business, and essentially total control, but that was all he would have. Control of something he didn't want without her. He had overplayed his hand. The master negotiator had failed. She had won. And they both lost in the end.

He looked subdued when he left a few minutes later, with much to think about. He looked at her longingly and wanted to kiss her, but he didn't dare.

Spencer met with Marcy and Paul the next morning and told them what she'd done.

"I took the deal," she said sadly.

"What deal?" Paul looked confused. "Did they offer us a new deal?" He looked hopeful.

"No, it's the deal I turned down before. I give up forty percent of my ownership the first year, another twenty percent the second year, and twenty again at the end of the second year. He reduced it to fifteen percent, which would give them seventy-five percent ownership within two years, and majority control after the first year. I refused the ten-year management contract they offered me. I don't want it. I couldn't do a good job for them once they own me. They offered me seven hundred and fifty thousand dollars a year for ten years, which would give me financial security for a decade. I don't care. I don't want it. They would own me like a slave, and once they have majority control, you know they'll change everything."

"They'd probably fire all of us," Marcy said. Paul

was shocked that Spencer had accepted the rest of it. She was giving up, beaten by events.

"Maybe I should just sell them the whole thing outright. It won't be the same after this. But I told him I'd only work for them for the first year to help them set it up. But after that I'd leave and it's their baby."

"What did he say?" Marcy asked her.

"He said he'd have to think about it."

"Do you really want to accept those terms?" Paul asked her.

"No, I don't. That's why I turned him down before and was willing to fight to the death. But too much has happened now. We really have no choice. It's pathetic. It took me seven years to destroy what my grandfather took sixty-two years to build. Even my father didn't do as much damage in four years as I have, and he did a pretty lousy job, and never liked the business. I've put my heart and soul into it, and look where we end up."

"It's not your fault, Spence." Paul tried to reassure her. "Times have changed. You can't fight the deterioration of the neighborhood to this degree. If your grandfather could have guessed there would be a drug war here on our doorstep and in the store, he'd never have bought here. Between the fire and this, and the importance of the internet, it really is too much. So, what happens next?" Paul asked her.

"We sign the deal when he draws up the papers, and that's it." She was ready to sign away her life, and the company she loved.

Spencer went to see two more temporary locations with Marcy that afternoon that were even worse than all the ones they had seen so far.

She was thinking about Mike as they rode back to the office in the darkened store with the boarded-up windows. They were waiting for the new ones to arrive, unless they left them that way when they put the building on the market to sell.

"He kissed me the other night," she said in a soft voice in the cab, and Marcy stared at her.

"Who did?"

"Mike. I cut my arm after the shootout when I went into the store to check on things. He went to the hospital with me when I got stitched up."

"You never said you got hurt. And what was he doing there?"

"He came to look for me when he figured out where I was. He called me. I was there in the side street while the shooting was going on."

"You never told us that either." Marcy was staring at her intently, and at the dazed look on Spencer's face.

"He spent the night in a chair, watching me

sleep when I got home, to make sure I was okay. He kissed me when he put me to bed."

"And sat watching you all night? And didn't sleep with you?" Marcy said, and Spencer nodded.

"For God's sake, he's in love with you. That's why he made you the offer he did in the first place. This deal is nothing compared to the investments he normally makes. I've read about him on the internet. The man is considered a financial genius. The last thing he needs is a small department store. I'm surprised his investors even let him do it. He usually makes billions for his investors on his deals. He won't with this. It's all about you, Spencer. Now it makes sense. It didn't to me before."

"Why not?" Spencer looked surprised.

"Because there isn't enough money in this deal for him and his investors. It's peanuts to them. This was all about you from the beginning. And if he kissed you and didn't sleep with you the other night, I can tell you for sure the man is in love with you. Men don't sleep with you when they love you, but they do sleep with you without a second thought when they don't. It's ass-backward, but that's how they are. He could have had sex with you the other night after the hospital, and he didn't. Instead, he sat up all night in a chair and watched you. Now it makes total sense, and he's not going to want seventy-five or eighty percent ownership of your store without you. That ten-year contract was practically a marriage proposal. He won't want this deal without you. I'm sure of it."

"You don't think he kissed me to make me take the deal?" Spencer asked.

"Absolutely not," Marcy replied.

"So, what do we do now?" Spencer asked her, looking baffled, but Marcy was a very smart woman, and she was usually right.

"You wait. That's all you do. For him to come out of the woods where he's hiding and declare himself like a man. And if he doesn't, you don't want him anyway. But I think he will, and you'll be hearing from him soon." Marcy sat back in the cab with a smug look on her face, and Spencer laughed.

"I think you're crazy, Marcy Parker. But I hope you're right. If you're not, I just handed him my grandfather's business on a silver platter, and I'm out of a job."

"Don't worry, you're not." Marcy patted Spencer's hand, and looked out the window with a knowing smile.

Chapter 14

Spencer spent the morning in her old office at the store, thinking about her exchange with Mike the day before. Marcy and Paul were in their offices too, and their secretaries had come in. The rest of the store was empty. There wasn't a sound in the building, and Spencer left her office to walk through the silent store, going from floor to floor, remembering her grandfather and the many times she had walked the building with him, and the wise things he had told her. She sat down on a couch in the designer dress department, laid her head back, and closed her eyes. She could almost feel her grandfather standing next to her and hear him in her head.

"Fight for what you believe in, Spencer," he always told her. "Never give up." "Don't sell yourself short." "Even if you're the only one left standing, keep fighting." And she hadn't. She had given up, and given in to Mike the day before. She was handing over the store to him and everything it meant to her. She couldn't let that happen, but she had.

There was no sensible way for them to stay in their location. She could no longer protect the building from what the neighborhood had become. She had to move forward with the times, she knew that too, and instead she had handed it all to Mike and was willing to walk away. She had given up. She had let the flame go out, in herself. She hadn't signed the deal yet, but she had given him her word. She was willing to give him seventy-five percent ownership in the business, and he didn't deserve it. No one did. He hadn't built it, she had, and her family had. The store was seventy-three years of her family's history, and she was letting it slip away. She was ashamed. And what would she tell her sons one day? What would she teach them? To fight? To hold on? To be strong and brave, or to give up and run away? She was running and she knew it was wrong. But how was she going to find a new building? Where would she find the money? She had nothing to sell except a store full of beautiful objects. But she didn't have enough to buy a new building, or even lease one. And moving uptown or downtown would be so expensive. She kept trying to think of a way out that didn't mean giving up three quarters of her business to Mike Weston and his investors. They were going to ruin everything.

When the store was gone, all she'd have left was her project for the homeless. She had emailed the others who had helped her, and they were meeting at the garage that night to hand out the new shipment on schedule. The others had gone there the night before to pack the bags. The bags were ready to hand out, and she had told the team she'd be there. She wasn't in the mood to see anyone. She had failed. She had nothing to be proud of. But that was no reason to deprive people who so desperately needed help and what she had to give them.

She went back to her office and sat at her grandfather's desk and felt unworthy of it. She felt humbled by everything that had happened, and everything she'd done, and all her mistakes. She didn't feel worthy of the legacy her grandfather had left her. She felt like a failure.

And so did Mike Weston. He had called his father that morning to ask if he knew of a building. Max always had good ideas, and sometimes he knew about unusual deals. He was the master of hidden treasures and ingenious solutions, which was the reason for his success.

"What kind of building?" Max Weston asked his son.

"Unusual, beautiful, elegant, for a very high-end specialty store," Mike explained.

"You're dabbling in fashion again? That's risky business." It was one kind of investment that had never appealed to Max, although his wife loved it. "There's a house on the market unofficially right now that no one wants. It'll probably be torn down one day. I bought it as a foreclosure because I thought your mother would love it, and she told me I was crazy. It needs some work, but it's what you just described. I own it. I've tried to sell it a few times, and no one wants to be bothered. They take one look, roll their eyes, and leave."

"You never told me about it."

"I forget about it. I felt stupid after I bought it. Your mother told me I had delusions of grandeur. She's probably right. And you know your mother, she likes modern." They had bought an ultramodern triplex in a new building instead, on the fiftieth floor. And they loved it. It was grandeur of another sort.

"Where is this place?" Mike was curious.

"On Fifth Avenue, squeezed between two apartment buildings. You don't even notice it as you drive by. It's grand inside, but relatively discreet outside. It's a hundred-twenty-year-old mansion, six blocks down from the Met. One of the Vanderbilts built it in 1900, and then moved to Newport."

"And Mom didn't want it?" Mike was surprised.

"It's dark inside. She loves lots of light." They had three-hundred-and-sixty-degree views of the city in their apartment. It was a whole different style. "You'd have to put in a lot of lighting."

"I don't think that matters. It's for a store," Mike reminded him. "Most stores don't have daylight."

"The house has had nine lives, as a museum, as an embassy, and a school. I don't think a family has lived in it since they built it."

"Can I see it?" Mike asked him. He had been sitting in his office brooding, thinking of his meeting with Spencer the day before. He felt guilty for what he had gotten her to agree to, giving up three quarters' ownership of her family legacy. And she had eluded him completely by refusing the management contract for more than a year. So, what was the point? And what did he want out of it anyway? He wasn't sure.

Max Weston looked at his watch. He had a lunch date at one, but he was free until then. "I could meet you there now."

"Do you mind? The store owners have needed to move for a long time and haven't faced up to it. There was a shooting in the store the other night, six people killed. Now they have to move in a hurry."

"You're buying the store?" Max sounded surprised.

"No, they need money to expand. I was going to invest in it. I made a deal for seventy-five percent ownership, and now it sounds crazy, and I feel guilty. It's a family business. I feel like I'm robbing the woman who owns it." His father listened carefully and didn't comment.

"We'll discuss it when I meet you." Max gave him the address, and twenty minutes later Mike arrived in a cab at the same time as his father pulled up with his driver in a Bentley.

"I like your car, Dad," he teased him. His father looked a great deal like him, except his hair was white and he wasn't as tall.

"Every time I buy a car that I like, your mother takes it. Now she wants this one." Max loved grumbling about his wife of nearly fifty years. Mike knew they adored each other. They had the kind of marriage he had always wanted, but he had made a terrible mistake with Maureen. His parents enjoyed their life together. They had fun, they had common interests. They worked on things together, they admired each other. They bought houses and sold them, and had friends. And they were proud of each other. Maureen had never been proud of

him, not for an instant. She had resented him almost since the beginning.

"Thank you for meeting me, Dad," Mike said
gratefully.

"Your mother called this my folly. Let's hope I
remember how to turn off the alarm." Max un-
locked the front door, punched in a code, and the
alarm was turned off. "Everything is either your
birthday or your sister's. This one is yours." Mike
smiled at him. He felt like it was a sign from the
universe that this house his father had bought and
couldn't get rid of was standing vacant. It didn't
look enormous from the outside, but as soon
as they walked into it, Mike saw that it was. It was
wide, although it looked dwarfed by the buildings
on either side, and it went far to the back of a large
lot, with a garden behind the house. There was a
grand marble staircase, and several large rooms off
the main entrance hall. There were five floors, and
each looked enormous. The original chandeliers
were in the house. The kitchen was antiquated, and
there were countless marble bathrooms. It was
confusing, but to Mike, looking around, it appeared to be about twice the size of the current
Brooke's home, and ten times more elegant. It
was an exquisite mansion in a perfect location,
it was empty, and his father owned it.

"How much do you want for it, Dad?" Mike asked him, as they got back to the main floor. The building had an elevator, and there were beautiful antique curtains at the windows. Mike thought it would make an incredibly elegant store.

"I have no idea. I got it for very little. The bank sold it when the school folded and defaulted on the payments."

"How long have you owned it?"

Max thought about it for a minute. "Maybe twenty years. You and Stephanie were both out of college, and your mother couldn't see us living here alone."

"It is a little grand," Mike admitted. "But perfect for what I have in mind. Would you rent it?"

"Maybe. So, who is this woman you're feeling guilty about? What store?"

"It's a place called Brooke's, downtown, in the wrong part of Chelsea."

"Where that drug war happened a few days ago?" Mike nodded. "I know the store. Interesting place. I went there a few times, but it's too much trouble to go down there. I knew the woman's father. Kind of a sad, dreary guy. He was a member of my club. Hated his job. I think he ran the place for a while and was embarrassed by it. I met his father once. He was on fire, terrific guy. He'd be about a hundred years old by now. This must be his granddaughter," Max Weston mused.

"It is." His father looked at him thoughtfully and got straight to the point.

"Are you in love with her?" Mike started to formulate a roundabout answer because he wasn't sure himself if he was, but he was beginning to think so.

"I might be."

"You are or you aren't. If you are, you don't need seventy-five percent of her family business. You don't need an excuse, just tell her. And if you don't love her, the last thing you need is seventy-five percent ownership of a store. It's a headache you don't need." Mike laughed. He had always loved how honest and direct his father was, and how brave. "You made a mistake once, don't make another one." His parents had never liked Maureen, and she didn't like them.

"This woman isn't a mistake, Dad. She's incredible."

"That's what you deserve. You're a good guy, Mike. And you're brave in business. Be brave with your heart too. That's never a mistake, even if you get hurt."

"She won't hurt me, Dad. She's a good person. I think I just hurt her with this stupid deal I offered her. She's got her back to the wall, so she accepted it. I feel terrible about it."

"Then clean it up." Mike nodded.

"I will."

"I'll rent the house to her if she wants it. She can buy it when she can afford to." Mike smiled and he hugged his father.

"Thank you, Dad. She's going to be the happiest woman alive when she sees this."

"She'd better make you the happiest man alive, or I'll evict her," Max said, and dropped the keys into his son's hand. "Bring her to look at it and see what she thinks. We can figure out the rent later. You make the deal. The place doesn't need much work. It's in pretty good shape, except for the kitchen."

They left the house together and Mike felt as though a miracle had happened. The building was like an answer from the Universe. He couldn't wait to show it to Spencer. He called her from the cab on the way back to his office, and she didn't pick up. He left her a message to call him. He was sure she'd call him back promptly, as she always did. He had appointments all afternoon, and kept checking his phone for messages, and there were none from Spencer. He picked Zack up at Maureen's and took him home. Zack could see immediately that Mike was in a good mood, that the darkness of the days before had lifted.

"I saw your grandfather today, he said to say

hello. You should call him sometime," Mike said to his son.

"I was waiting to get my casts off. I can't get around with the stupid wheelchair."

"I'll take you to see him," Mike promised, and tried Spencer again.

She had seen his calls come in, and she was sure he wanted her to sign the papers for the deal she'd agreed to, and she was in no hurry to do it. She felt like a traitor every time she thought of it, but she had given her word, so she would do it. It would be one of the worst days of her life when she signed.

She left her office and had dinner with her boys, and then went to the garage to meet the others. She got there at seven and checked the bags. Everyone was there, even though the store was closed. They had showed up to hand out the bags they had loaded the night before. She thanked everyone for coming and was lining the bags up on a table near the entrance when she saw Mike walk in, in jeans and a sweatshirt. He looked serious when his eyes met hers.

"I thought maybe you could use a spare pair of hands. I didn't know if everyone would show up."

"They did, but thank you for coming," she said politely.

"I called you today and left you messages. You

didn't call me back." It was a statement more than a reproach.

"I know. I'm sorry. I was busy. I was going to call you later." He suspected that she wasn't going to, and he didn't blame her. The heartbreak of what she'd agreed to was in her eyes. He had become her enemy overnight, because of the deal he'd offered her. But she was angrier at herself than at him. To him, it was just business.

Their first customer drifted in then, and one of the team members handed him a bag and wished him a good night.

"I thought maybe the garage would be closed too because of what happened the other night," the man said, and Spencer stepped in to assure him the garage would be open on schedule.

"That's nice of you," the man said softly, and left with his bag. Others like him drifted in, and the garage got crowded very quickly, as the team handed out bags with clothing in the right sizes. Their last customer came in at ten, and they only had nine bags left. It had been a good night and the workers from Brooke's were smiling and pleased. They helped themselves to the dough-nuts, and Spencer offered them to Mike. She had cheered up as the evening wore on. She loved what they were doing, and Mike smiled at her. It had been a good night for him too. It warmed his heart just being there with her. He loved what she did there.

"I have a lot to tell you," he said quietly, as they got ready to leave. "Can we go somewhere to talk?" He looked hopeful and she hesitated.

"I don't want to talk business tonight," she said gently. "It's been a long day and I'm tired." She looked it, but more than anything she looked sad, and he knew he had done that.

"There are some things I need to say to you," he said, and she nodded.

"There's a coffee shop two blocks from here. We can walk there." He followed her out and she locked up as the others left too, and Mike walked toward the coffee shop with her. She and Mike took a booth in the back, and she ordered an iced tea, and Mike ordered coffee. He was tired too. He'd had a lot to think about and had hardly slept the night before. He started talking before their drinks came. He couldn't wait any longer.

"I want to apologize for the deal I offered you yesterday. I don't want seventy-five percent owner-ship of your business, Spencer. I rescind the offer. I'm not going to do it with my investors. They wouldn't understand it anyway. I'm not sure I do, but I'd like to try. I don't know what I was thinking. I don't need to make the best deal here. This isn't Wall Street. It's your legacy from your grandfather.

I want to offer you something very different. I'm going to do this with my own money. If you're willing, I'd like to buy forty-nine percent of the business, and you keep fifty-one percent. If you like the way we work together, at the end of a year, or two years if you like that better, I'd like to buy one percent from you, so that we each own fifty percent, as equal partners. I want to be a working partner with you, and help you build the business. I'd like to do it together. You can teach me the business, and I can help you make good financial decisions. And if you don't like the way we work together, you keep the fifty-one percent, and keep the controlling interest in the business. And if I turn out to be a complete jerk, I'll sell you back the forty-nine percent, and you'll be rid of me forever." She smiled when he said it.

"That's not what I want. I like the idea of being working partners. What made you change your mind?" Spencer was curious about Mike's decision. The proposition he'd just made sounded interesting to her.

"My conscience and my father, in that order," he answered her.

"I like your new offer better." She smiled broadly at him. "I was going to sign because I gave you my word."

"You're an honorable woman, and a worthy

opponent." He smiled back at her and took her hand in his and held it.

"I like the idea of being working partners. Even equal partners, if you behave," she said, feeling brave, and then her face grew serious again. "There's only one problem, we don't have a store."

"That's debatable," Mike said. "My father is something of a wild card and a little crazy. I love him. He buys businesses and houses, he has unusual ideas, and they always end up making money. He always has something up his sleeve, or a rabbit in his pocket. I called him today to see if he knew of any properties to rent or buy that would work for a store. He told me that he bought a mansion twenty years ago that my mother hated, and he never sold it. He still owns it, and it's just been sitting there for twenty years, unoccupied. I went to look at it with him, and it's gorgeous. It's perfect for Brooke's and about twice the size of what you have now, which seems like the right expansion to me, without branches in every city. It's at Seventy-sixth and Fifth, and he gave me the keys so I can show you. He'll rent it to us for whatever we want." Her eyes grew wide as she listened to him. It sounded like a dream come true. The past few days had been a nightmare, and overnight it had changed.

"Are you serious?" she whispered. The location

was fantastic. And his description of it. "When can we see it?"

"Whenever you want, since I have the keys. Tomorrow morning if you're free."

"Are you kidding? I'll be there at sunrise."

"I'll pick you up at eight-thirty. I honestly think it's the answer to a prayer. I can't wait till you see it." He was grinning broadly and hadn't let go of her hand. "My father is always full of surprises. And there's one other thing. What's your position on dating your business partner? Do you have a policy on that?"

"I've never had a business partner before." She smiled at him. "I think it's an excellent idea though. We ought to try it."

"I wholeheartedly agree. I think we should start with dinner on Saturday night to celebrate."

"Very good policy. I second that." She was still smiling. "When do we sign the papers?"

"Wait till you see the house first, and make sure you like it and think it will work as a store. We can rent it for now and buy it later if we want."

"How did all this happen?" She looked at him in amazement.

"I think it's because you're magic," he whispered to her, and she laughed.

They saw the house together the next morning,

and Spencer couldn't believe how beautiful it was. It was the perfect setting for Brooke's, much more than the old store had been. She kept thanking Mike as she walked from room to room, and when she finally stopped long enough, in her excitement to see every inch of it, he put his arms around her and held her close and kissed her for the second time since the carnage at the store.

"You've made all my dreams come true," she whispered to him. "I don't deserve this."

"Oh yes, you do," he said firmly, and kissed her again. "We both do. It took us a long time to get here, and I'm going to enjoy every minute of it with you."

They walked through the house a second time, while she made careful notes and sketches, and took pictures. She agreed with his father. There wasn't a lot of work to do. She was guessing that they could get it up and running in three months, by the fall. They would have to work like crazy to do it, but hard work never scared her. It wasn't far from Mike's office on Park Avenue, and he said he could meet her at the store for lunch when he was free.

They hated to leave, but they had a lot to do now. She had to decide if she wanted to keep the old location open till they moved, or close while they worked on the new location and focus on that. Mike was going to provide the operating funds to get the new location set up as a store.

"Why don't we figure out how much money you'll lose if you close the old store now, or if it makes more sense to keep it open. I'll work up the numbers with Paul Trask, and we can decide. What are you doing on Sunday by the way?"

"I have the boys," she reminded him, "with no nanny."

"I was thinking we could take them for a walk on the Chelsea Piers with Zack. It's nice level ground for his wheelchair, and I'd like him to meet them, and you." She smiled as they got into a cab together. She was going to drop him off at his office, and head downtown to tell the others what had happened. The whole world had changed in a single day, thanks to Mike.

He kissed her as the cab sped down Fifth Avenue and turned toward Park Avenue a few blocks down.

"I'm very happy with our policy about working partners," he whispered to her, and she laughed.

"So am I."

Chapter 15

When Spencer got to the office, she rounded up Marcy, Beau, and Paul, and had them come to her office. She explained the new arrangement with Mike, that she was retaining majority control, but that at some later date, if she chose to, she and Mike would become equal partners, at her discretion. And then she told them about the mansion Mike's father was going to rent to her. She showed them the photos she'd taken on her phone, and they were as astonished as she had been. They loved the location, and the interiors. They were going to put the restaurant at ground level this time, and use the garden for outdoor dining in summer. Spencer had a million ideas about where to put each department, in all the rooms that had been previously used as bedrooms or sitting rooms, the main dining room, the elegant living room, with space for all their offices upstairs. It was going to be the most beautiful specialty store in New York.

And Paul and Mike got to work deciding if Brooke's should stay open downtown for the summer, or close until they opened uptown. There were a million decisions to be made.

Spencer called the realtor and put the store in Chelsea on the market. They would have to disclose the shootout that had occurred there. Spencer couldn't guess who would buy it, or how they would use it, and even though Brooke's had an elegant new home to go to, she knew she would be sad when it sold. It would mean leaving a big part of her history behind.

On Saturday night Mike took Spencer to Le Bernardin, one of the best restaurants in the city. He ordered champagne, and when he took her home they tiptoed upstairs to her bedroom and locked the door to her suite. He smiled when he saw the chair where he had spent the night watching her after the shootout. They marveled at how life could change in an instant. Everything was different now. When they made love for the first time, with the moonlight streaming into her bedroom, she felt as though she had been waiting for him all her life, and her past faded behind her like so much mist as she lay in his arms afterwards. She didn't let him spend the night because Axel and Ben were home, and he had Zack staying at his apartment.

"We have to go somewhere for a weekend," he said, sad to leave her.

"The boys go on sleepovers," she reminded him, and he laughed. They were refugees from their children. He wanted her to meet his parents, and so did she. She had a great deal to thank his father for, and she was interested to meet his mother and learn about her online fashion business that was a worldwide success, and his sister Stephanie who worked for her. She warned him about her mother, who found fault with everything and disapproved of everything Spencer did. They had much to learn about each other, and new worlds to discover.

On Sunday, she took Axel and Ben to meet Mike and Zack at the Chelsea Piers. The twins loved it, and ran alongside Zack's wheelchair trying to make him guess which one was which, and were delighted when he got it wrong. They ate ice cream, and went out for pizza afterwards, and Zack promised to take them to the batting cages at the Pier when he got his casts off. They were very impressed that he'd been hit by a bus.

"I think that went very smoothly," Mike said after dinner, as he and Spencer left the restaurant to join the boys waiting for them outside.

"The boys think Zack is a hero. He let them both sign his cast," Spencer said. The twins had been starving for male companionship for so long that they basked in the warmth of Zack and Mike's attention. Ben was the more outgoing of the two and had an affinity for Zack. Axel was quieter, talked to Mike all afternoon and stayed close to him, telling him all about his special reading classes at school. And Mike guessed correctly twice which twin was which, which impressed Spencer. Usually, no one could tell them apart except her.

"Ben's smile is just a tiny bit bigger, and he has laughing eyes," he said to her.

"You pay attention."

"Yes, I do," he said quietly, and gently touched her cheek. "I can't wait for you to meet Jennifer too, she'll be home in a few weeks. She's already obsessed with you."

"I haven't forgotten her discount," Spencer said, and he laughed. "Wait till she sees the new store." There was going to be an open house for realtors at the old store the following Sunday. Their realtor was going to list it with international brokers all over the world.

There was so much to look forward to now. And so much to do.

The following week Mike rented a house in the Hamptons for two weeks in August, so they could all spend time together. He had checked it out with Maureen, who was going to Europe to meet friends in Capri, so the timing worked for her. He suspected there was a new man involved but didn't ask her. They had almost settled the financial part of their divorce. It had been costly but well worth it. They were both happier and getting along better than they had in years, and he had been generous with her. She got the house in Connecticut, which she was going to sell, and the apartment in the city, most of the art, but not all, and a handsome settlement, and he was paying all the kids' expenses, including college and apartments when they graduated. The divorce would be final at the end of the year.

Mike and Spencer went to the lawyer to sign their agreement together. It was a serious moment and Spencer almost cried when she signed it.

Spencer, Beau, and Marcy went to the house on Fifth Avenue almost daily, with the architect, the construction crew, a decorator, and a lighting specialist. Spencer was taking all the art from the old location and had already removed it and put it in storage so it didn't get stolen, and they were building new cabinetry to show the merchandise to its best advantage. There were no windows on the street this time, but lots of display cases inside, and having the store in a mansion made it seem even more exclusive. She thought her grandparents would have loved it.

The following Sunday, they had dinner at Mike's parents' spectacular apartment. Beverly and Max invited Spencer to bring the twins with her, and Mike brought Zack to see his grandparents. They had a home theater, and Max put on a movie for the kids, and they loved it. And Beverly made popcorn for them. Overnight, Spencer and the twins had inherited a family, with older siblings and grandparents, and Max gave his son a thumbs-up of approval while Beverly was explaining to Spencer about her internet business, and how it had started, small at first, and mammoth now. Some of her best markets were in Asia.

It came as a shock to Spencer in July when the realtor emailed her and said they had a serious prospect for the store. He was willing to pay their full asking price. The prospective buyer was from

Singapore and wanted to turn the building into an exclusive boutique hotel. He intended to add a large security staff and set up a night patrol, which would benefit the neighborhood and make it safer. And so far his financial references had checked out, and he had agreed to their terms and was going to buy all the fixtures they were willing to leave behind. Spencer wanted to keep the iconic, historical ones. Spencer had mixed feelings about the sale as soon as she read the email. On the one hand, she wanted to sell it, and needed to, but on the other hand, it would be bittersweet when it sold.

In mid-July, Zack's casts came off, and he had to do rehab for his wrists and his leg. He was stiff from being unable to use them. He was diligent about the rehab so he could play sports again. The five of them went to the park, and he threw a ball around with the twins, and Mike joined them while Spencer watched and lay on a blanket on the grass. They had brought a picnic with them and spent the day there before they went back downtown.

And it was cause for celebration when Jennifer finally came home in July and met Spencer. Spencer took her to see the new store in progress, and Jennifer was in awe when she saw it, and loved spending time with her. They went shopping to-gether and Spencer took her to lunch. Mike loved to see them get along. He was doing better with Maureen these days, who was in a much better mood. She had a new boyfriend, and was happy about the divorce now. She had forgotten what it felt like to be happy, after years of being married to a man she didn't love anymore.

And at the center of it all, Spencer and Mike were happy and in love. They were worthy opponents, lovers, partners, and friends. The relationship gave them each what they wanted and had given them a new life. And his clever structure of their association made it feel like a partnership from the start.

"I really like her, Dad," Jennifer told Mike shortly after she got back from San Francisco. She was staying with Mike more than with her mother. She and Maureen had a relatively peaceful truce for the moment, but she didn't want to push it.

Spencer took both Zack and Jenny with her to the Free Love garage when they asked her to, and they helped her hand out the bags. Zack even vol-unteered for an evening of filling them, and said he really liked the crew. Mike came with her every week when she went there.

* * *

They had decided to keep the old store closed for the summer while they focused on the new one. The HR people were busy hiring additional employees for the larger store, while the ones who had worked in Chelsea were off for the summer on half pay, and most of them were happy to have the time off. A few complained, but not many.

And for Spencer and Mike, the future was glittering ahead of them, beckoning them forward like stars in a brightly lit summer sky. They had fought hard for their dreams, as opponents and allies, and they had both won in the end.

Chapter 16

On the fourteenth of September, the car parkers in starched white jackets were lined up ready to take charge of the cars on Fifth Avenue. Most of the guests arrived with their cars and drivers. Two hundred people had accepted the invitation to discover the new store. The women emerged from their cars in short cocktail dresses and high heels, with impressive jewels. They were among the most elegant women in New York, wearing big-name designers and Parisian haute couture. They were all desperate to come inside and see the store. Liveried waiters were serving champagne on silver trays, with hors d'oeuvres by the best caterer in New York. The flowers in enormous urns placed in effective locations were spectacular, and people were in awe of the magnificent mansion with well-chosen furnishings in inviting groupings. There was soft music playing and the scent of delicate perfume in the air. People were going up and down the staircase, and stopping at every floor to discover where to find their favorite items.

Marcy was wearing a chic black dress, the men were all in coats and ties. Spencer was wearing a short red lace dress with long sleeves and a plunging back to the waist. The mayor had come, the editors of **Vogue** and **Harper's Bazaar,** and all the right journalists from **WWD** and **The Business of Fashion** online. There was a photographer from the **New York Post** combing the crowd for famous faces, of which there were many. Rappers wearing all their bling, politicians, writers, movie stars. The crowd was even more exciting than the clothes, and the details of the house were enhanced by being freshly painted. No one was disappointed by what they saw that night. For those who had forgotten that Brooke's existed, it was a lively reminder, and for those who had never known it, it was an introduction they wouldn't soon forget. There were TV reporters and members of the fashion and mainstream press.

Spencer watched the crowd arrive and knew that the evening was a success before it even started. The atmosphere was electric and warm and excited.

Mike found her and asked her to come to his office. He had to tell her something important. She was waiting for him there when he walked in, looking incredibly handsome in a dark suit, a white shirt, and the Hermès tie she had given him. He put his arms around her when he walked in and kissed her, and she smiled.

"It all looks great, doesn't it?" she said happily.

"Of course, because you did it," he complimented her. His parents were coming later, and she couldn't wait for them to see it.

"What did you want to tell me?" she asked, curious as to why he wanted to see her in his office, and he smiled.

"I just wanted to tell you that I love you," he said and kissed her, "so we don't forget what this event is about and how lucky we are." It reminded him of the evening when he had invited her to the party at the Met, and seeing her before that, at the store, when she greeted him so politely. He had dozens of images of her in his mind now, of different places and times. They had been through some hard times together, and some terrifying moments, the nights of the fire and the shooting, and happy moments alone and with their children. The contract she had agreed to and almost signed, and the one they finally did sign, which had brought them together for this magically beautiful event. It felt almost like a wedding and was the celebration of the bond between them now, both personal and professional. When they had dined at the Met, Spencer had never expected any of this to happen, that she would be the woman in his arms one day, and the person she would share the new store and her life with, as well as her history.

What she had learned in the months of working with Mike, in the hard times and the good times, was what a remarkable person he was, and he had learned the same about her. They were a perfectly matched couple, where each moment together was a graceful dance. And they had fun together too.

He kissed her one last time in the privacy of his handsomely done wood-paneled office in the old library, and then they went back downstairs to enjoy the guests and continue to show them around for the rest of the evening.

When they went back to the party, Spencer heard a voice behind her speak above the others. "The lights are too bright, because the ceiling fixtures are too low." She laughed the moment she heard it and turned to see her mother. She knew it had to be her. Only she could find fault in an evening like this. But Eileen seemed to be enjoying herself, speaking to an older couple who were newly arrived. They were telling her about their latest cruise. They had gone halfway around the world. Eileen's eyes lit up when she spoke to them, and then she glanced over at her daughter with a shy smile. Spencer couldn't imagine that it was a sign of approval, but anything was possible on a night like this.

There was a small area with a dance floor set up, and Mike danced with Spencer for a few minutes and then stopped to say good night to their guests as they left.

People stayed late that night. The last guest left just after midnight, although the invitation had said "until ten." It was a dazzling success, and old and new customers couldn't wait to shop there. And there was a long mention of the party on Page Six of the **Post** the next day.

The day after the party, the realtor called Spencer to remind her that the old store would be coming out of escrow shortly, and she wanted to give Spencer an opportunity to say goodbye to it if she wanted to. It seemed like a foolish gesture, but it meant a great deal to Spencer. So much of her life had been spent at the store in Chelsea. So many wonderful things had happened there, so many people she loved had been there before her, so many dreams had been born in that building, and so many people had been touched by what happened there. Her life and her future had taken form in that store, and even the lives of her children were touched by it.

She quietly walked through the building remembering the events that had taken place, the precious moments that had touched her life forever, the people she had loved who were the essence of it.

She thought she would be leaving them all behind when she sold it, but as she stood there, she realized that she was taking them with her. She had thought that the magic was in the structure in Chelsea, only to discover that it was within her, woven into the tapestry of her life and her being. And now new people had come into her life and were part of the magic too.

By some miracle, she and Mike had found each other, and had traveled their lifetimes to get here. Worthy opponents, beloved friends, loving partners, and together, they were taking the magic with them and adding to it with new memories and adventures.

* * *

Her footsteps echoed in the hall as she walked to the front door for the last time, turned, and looked at the building, imprinting the memories on her heart.

And then she walked through the front door and closed it softly behind her.

Mike was waiting for her outside, and he looked into her eyes when she came out.

"Ready?" he asked her, and she nodded. He knew how hard it had been for her to sell it, but so much lay ahead of them now, so much to look forward to. She remembered her grandfather's words, "Never be afraid of change."

"Ready," she answered in a strong, clear voice, as he put an arm around her, and they walked down the street together. She looked up at him and smiled, and he pulled her closer. He had protected her, and she had been brave for him. They had proven that they were worthy of each other. Her grandfather would have been so proud, as they walked down the street into their future, taking the legacy with them like a blessing.

About the Author

DANIELLE STEEL has been hailed as one of the world's bestselling authors, with almost a billion copies of her novels sold. Her many international bestsellers include **Without a Trace, The Whittiers, The High Notes, The Challenge, Suspects, Beautiful, High Stakes, Invisible, Flying Angels,** and other highly acclaimed novels. She is also the author of **His Bright Light,** the story of her son Nick Traina's life and death; **A Gift of Hope,** a memoir of her work with the homeless; **Expect a Miracle,** a book of her favorite quotations for inspiration and comfort; **Pure Joy,** about the dogs she and her family have loved; and the children's books **Pretty Minnie in Paris** and **Pretty Minnie in Hollywood.**

daniellesteel.com
Facebook.com/DanielleSteelOfficial
Twitter: @daniellesteel
Instagram: @officialdaniellesteel

LIKE WHAT YOU'VE READ?

Try these titles by Danielle Steel,
also available in large print:

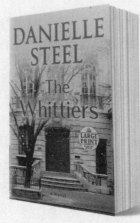

The Whittiers
ISBN 978-0-593-58784-3

Without a Trace
ISBN 978-0-593-58785-0

The High Notes
ISBN 978-0-593-58783-6

For more information on large print titles, visit
www.penguinrandomhouse.com/large-print-format-books